BOOKWHACKED

BOOKWHACKED

A NOVEL

AUTHORS CRAZED TO SAVE THE WORLD

MICHAEL SCOFIELD

Sunstone books may be purchased for educational, business, or sales promotional use. For information please write: Special Markets Department, Sunstone Press, P.O. Box 2321, Santa Fe, New Mexico 87504-2321.

Book and cover design › Vicki Ahl
Body typeface › Palatino Linotype
Printed on acid-free paper
∞
eBook 978-1-61139-535-8

Library of Congress Cataloging-in-Publication Data

Names: Scofield, Michael, author.
Title: Bookwhacked : a novel : authors crazed to save the world / by Michael Scofield.
Description: Santa Fe : Published by Sunstone Press, [2018]
Identifiers: LCCN 2017053140 (print) | LCCN 2017057385 (ebook) | ISBN 9781611395358 | ISBN 9781632932105 (softcover : alk. paper)
Classification: LCC PS3619.C63 (ebook) | LCC PS3619.C63 B66 2018 (print) | DDC 813/.6--dc23
LC record available at https://lccn.loc.gov/2017053140

WWW.SUNSTONEPRESS.COM
SUNSTONE PRESS / POST OFFICE BOX 2321 / SANTA FE, NM 87504-2321 /USA
(505) 988-4418 / ORDERS ONLY (800) 243-5644 / FAX (505) 988-1025

To Noreen

Acknowledgments

Special thanks to Annie Woods for editing help.

Added thanks to Jim Smith and Carl Condit for sharing their experiences in the world of independent publishing.

I'm especially grateful to writers Mary Dezember, Richard Lehnert, Donald Levering, James McGrath, Barbara Rockman, Russel Stolins, and Robert Wilder for their friendship and encouragement.

Cast of Characters

Charlie Small: owner of Surely You Jest Press

Benjamin (Benji) LaForge: Charlie's assistant

Candace (Candy) Carlton: Charlie's Art Director

Jeannie LaForge: Benji's mother

Kittie Rehmeyer: Charlie's CPA, self-help author

Joe Tash: coauthor of *You Can Save Us All*

Jane Tash: coauthor of *You Can Save Us All*, Joe's wife

Hercules (Herk) O'Ryan: graphic artist, Jane's son

Seymour Sabatini: millionaire, poet

Vanessa Z. Nord: Seymour's girlfriend, poet

Marta Means: anthropologist, memoirist

Rolf (Mad Dog) Goodenough: best-selling author of westerns

Trevor Quesenberry: owner of Words, Words, Words bookstore

1

How It All Began

A year ago, on a hot Thursday afternoon in July, Joe and Jane Tash's five-year-old, Tatum, was building a sand castle between her seesaw and slide under a couple of maples. Her usual sitter, the neighbor's teenage daughter—supposed to be watching—was texting her best friend.

Upstairs, in the five-bedroom colonial that sat on an acre-plus in southern Connecticut, Jane had just rung off the phone, following Joe's news. Exaggerating her breath to calm her nerves, she stretched out on the queen-size, hospital-style bed they'd installed for Joe's back inside a canopied frame. Sweat built under her arms and between her thighs. She listened to Tatum's chirps through the screen, having switched off central air. Even before Joe's call, its whisper had started agitating her.

First she needed to talk to Hercules, her son by a first marriage. As strapping as she, Herk seemed to grouse, every time they spoke now, about the hours he put in as Creative Director at Mitchum, Bittle, & Rousseau, the country's leading ad agency specializing in mechanized farm equipment. Like the advertising-illustrator-turned-artist Edward Hopper, Herk wished to abandon Satan's gristmill, as he dubbed it, and, unlike Hopper, paint landscapes free of people.

First, phone Herk to take the train up from Manhattan for a celebratory dinner. Next, drive to Country Larder for a filet mignon, asparagus, and, ignoring Joe's diet, chocolate-drizzled cheesecake. The sitter had sworn to Jane that she would never again bring her smartphone, following Tatum's fall face first in the stream that gurgled across an untended corner of lawn. That time she had been texting her boyfriend and let Tatum wander.

Jane decided she'd better sit up, not to wrinkle further the blouse her cleaning woman had ironed yesterday. The Egyptian-cotton gift from Joe displayed peonies matching the red and pink blossoms coloring the Tashes' living-room and guest-bedroom windows, extending left and right from the front porch.

Later, to the Episcopalian priest, Jane recalled that her conversation with Herk went like this:

"Darling."

"I'm kinda busy here, Mom. Can we talk after dinner?"

"Dine with *us*, baby. Meet your train around six? Joe and I are blowing off the lid."

"Yeah?"

"Your father just got promoted to head up Goldman's commodity index and do a bit of fence-mending with the press."

"My *father*? Dad's managing the Hilton in Boston, last I heard, unless his drinking has swamped him."

"Not that father."

"Only got one."

"Herk, let's not start, okay? Joe would be so appreciative."

"He hates my guts."

"He does not *hate your guts*, Herk."

"Because I admire even less what *he's* doing than what I'm doing. Because I'm six foot two and he's shorter even than *you*. Because you and I are practicing Episcopalians. We walk the talk, Mom, do we not? Because I can't listen to his Excellency explain shorts and longs and futures more than five—"

"All *right*, Herk. Please: stay in the City."

"Pick me up at six, okay? I'll take the four fifty-three. Talmadge Hill or the New Canaan station?"

"Oh, wonderful, thank you, darling. Talmadge Hill—I'll be heading from home."

Perhaps that coming Saturday, Jane remembered thinking, Joe could find storage for his new outboard. It rested in the drive on its trailer in front of his side of the converted-carriage-house garage. He refused to leave his Z3 along the curb and walk, what, twenty feet to the porch? Too far for his nibs. From the Talmadge Hill station Joe insisted on driving smack up against her garage door, unfolding the custom-fitted tarp, and snugging it over the roadster, top down.

Considering the promotion, she felt sure he'd be itching to drive to Hartford on Saturday or Sunday to talk to the BMW dealer about trading the Z3 for a Z4. Not fair, having to wait while he backed his hot rod out of the way, when she needed to exit the garage. Why did he feel Tatum required the adventures implicit in her father owning a fiberglass boat, anyway? Joe knew, because of Jane's near death by drowning just past Tatum's age, that lakes terrified his wife.

No matter what you want, Joseph, *this* weekend we're finding storage for that souped-up skiff, Jane thought, and glanced at her watch.

From the kitchen's island she grabbed her purse, strode through the laundry, and out into the heat and ryegrass-scented air. She slapped dead a mosquito that had buried its dart in her forearm. She must have then shouted something like, "Carrie, that looks like an iPhone on your belt!" And the neighbor's daughter had lied, "Mom asked me to bring it, Mrs. Tash, she may need me home early." Jane had replied, "No taking off until I return from shopping, that's an hour max I need you here. Reminder: no texting."

"No, Mrs. Tash, I promise. My eyes stay locked on Tatum."

Jane remembered, then, dashing over. Just the weekend prior, giving in to Tatum's pleas, Joe had repainted her sandbox's blue boards yellow. Jane scooped her out and up. About to flick away the ladybug she spotted in the five-year-old's black curls, instead she left the insect there, a gift from God, and hugged tight her little miracle from an unplanned pregnancy, at age forty-three.

"Carrie's in charge, Tatum."

"Yes, Mama."

"I'll be home before your father arrives. He got a big promotion."

"What's 'promotion'?"

"He'll explain."

"Maybe he'll get here soon."

"Could be."

"To see me!"

"Of course to see you," Jane recalled laughing, and kissed her daughter's cheeks.

She hurried to the side door cut into the carriage house/garage, no doubt shook her head at the bicycles, toboggan, never-used-anymore lawn mower (the gardener brought his own), skis and poles, cartons holding Joe's jazz LPs—no room for the Z3. She slipped into her turbo wagon, set her purse on the cream-colored leather seat after removing her sunglasses and chain of keys, and punched the remote clipped to the visor.

The door began its grind upward. She strapped herself in, switched on ignition and air, and found herself stamping her foot waiting for the goddamned door. Though she did not like leaving Tatum behind, she could shop so much faster without the child yanking her hand to plead, in turn, for Doritos, Milk Duds, cupcakes, Oreos, Reese's Pieces, and donuts.

Unknown to Jane, Joe—impossible to concentrate following his boss's good news—had taken an early train. By the time the garage door had completed its rise, he'd swung the convertible, top stowed, off West onto Jonathan, and was careering into the long drive that swept toward the carriage-house garage.

Tatum heard the roar from her father's mufflers at the moment that Carrie heard a blast of heavy metal at her hip and pulled her smartphone from its holster.

As Jane glanced at her watch and tromped on the accelerator, and as Joe—about to foot the brake pedal— squealed left toward the retracted door, Tatum ran around the corner, able a single time to cry out, "Daddy!" before the rear of the Volvo and front of the Z3 crushed between them her thighs, pelvis, and lower rib cage.

Before her chin dropped to the sports car's hood, her lips stretched as though invisible fingers were prying them wide. The only sound, however, came from Jane who, having dared glance into the rearview, threw her hands to her sunglasses and shrieked. Harnessed into her seat, she started keening.

Joe unbuckled and, necktie flying, hurtled over the Z3's door. The vehicles had pinned his daughter where he couldn't reach, could only watch the blood pour from her mouth and button nose.

Carrie appeared, iPhone at her ear, and cried out. Joe grabbed the phone, punched *END*, and managed to reach 911 before collapsing to his knees on the cobblestones. "What the fuck, oh, what the, oh, fuck, what the," Jane remembered him stammering.

Carrie leapt the low fence and dashed over her mother's peonies toward their screen door.

When the ambulance arrived, Jane was still strapped in her Volvo. Joe was on the wooden bench beside the drive, pain stabbing his back, staring into the cluster of birch where the picnic table sat, blue-and-red tie knotted tight against his fleshy neck, drops of sweat plopping onto his collar. Though blood had soaked the visible parts of Tatum's pinafore, she seemed simply to be sleeping upright, head lolling, shoulders sagged.

Jane, tears streaking her makeup, had recalled to the priest how the orange ladybug, tossed to its back in one of Tatum's curls, kept fluttering its legs.

A month later, their daughter underground, Jane and Joe decided they must leave the East Coast. Encouraged by the marriage counselor they'd sought out, they also started brainstorming a book to write. Working title? *You Can Save Us All*. For Jane, who'd quickly become a Tea Party Patriot after Tatum passed, *You* meant God. For Joe, *You* meant the world's peoples.

2

Hustle, Hustle

In the news:

140,000-acre Jemez Mountains wildfire leaves skeletal trees, concrete slabs, black goop, melted pickups and SUVs. "We were surprised anything was left standing," said Guadalupe Lupa. "Nothing has come close to the size of this since my family settled here in 1921."

Yellowstone River, the only watercourse of size in the United States left undammed, rises above flood stage. US Wildlife Service crews grow increasingly concerned that 1,000 barrels of crude leaking from a 12-inch pipeline could poison the river's prized fishery.

President Obama's hopes to restrain deepening national debt have been squashed by Republicans' refusal to raise taxes in order to balance Democrats' push for spending cuts. "We must end this stalemate amicably, and soon," the President warns.

Long John Café's Tequila Cream Sauce Parfait called "scrumptious, moist, refreshing" by Long John's aunt, Mandy Claris. "My cousins and I were all licking the glass," she enthused. —Pasatiempo, restaurant review

"I like this," Charlie Small declared in Santa Fe a year after Tatum's death. The septuagenarian owner of New Mexico's largest commercial publisher, Surely You Jest Press, held up a hard copy of *You Can Save Us All*. Accompanied by a hesitant Herk, Joe and Jane had brought in the manuscript fifteen minutes ago for their appointment at ten.

The outside temperature already had reached eighty-three degrees. But inside the foot-thick adobe walls, Joe and Jane; Herk; Charlie; Charlie's assistant, Benji; and Surely You Jest's art director, Candace (Candy) Carlton, mostly were able to stay comfortable without air-conditioning.

Charlie's hundred-and-fifty-year-old building on the same street as the Georgia O'Keeffe Museum had started life as a Civil War barracks, became a nursing home, and for forty years had housed the press.

Benji, thirty-eight-years old, manned the front office. Candy struggled down the hall to stay current with updates for InDesign typographical software and PhotoShop, pumping out covers for the seventy or so titles per year the press published. Four days a week she ate a bologna sandwich and half an apple in the tiny courtyard, facing her office, in which she'd planted Russian hawthorn in half barrels brought from home. The July-reddening berries reminded her of picking cherries before leaving the Columbia River to marry her only, big-mistake husband.

On the courtyard's other side lay the cracked asphalt of the parking lot serving clients, brokers, and staff of Charlie Small's longtime lessee, Sotheby's International Realty.

Cedar siding defined the windowless office where Charlie, Joe, Jane, and Herk at present conferred. The two-hundred-plus Surely You Jest titles still in print, mostly southwestern history but also poetry, shoot-em-up novels, and travel guides, filled a wall of shelves behind the Tashes. On a table fashioned from mesquite beside Charlie's desk sat framed headshots, not of the press's best-known authors but photos of those who, as Charlie put it, "Never turned rancid on me."

Charlie claimed he stayed peppy by letting "a ton of anger boil off in regular sequence." He kept a full crop of gray hair dyed sienna and wore an Old Miss class ring resized for his pinky.

From his swivel chair, Charlie peered between twin monitors on his left and a stack of black-bound *Britannicas* on his right at the couple who'd moved with her son—hunched with them on the couch—six months ago from New Canaan to Tesuque. The cracks in Joe's leather watchband annoyed Charlie, as did the strands of hair that had fallen along Jane's cheek. But he liked that Joe's corduroy cargo shorts were creased, looking as expensive as his madras shirt—and that the patches-of-green on Jane's shirtdress matched the color of the spines of the five-volume *Female Martyrs of the West: Native, Hispanic, Anglo*, one of Surely You Jest's best sellers.

"You two," Charlie said, "as I thumbed the first few pages, have come up with a concept sorely needed; you're persuasive writers."

"Joe's more," Jane said, glancing sideways at her husband.

"Oh, the hell I am."

"Agreed." Having left on his Stetson, Herk lifted a boot to droop off the knee of his jeans. Since decamping from Manhattan in January, the late-twenties graphic designer had added a paunch that folded over his belt.

"Herk," Jane cautioned.

Wrangling already, Charlie thought, and called out, "Benji, where's that coffee?" To the trio, he said, "Benji's a lifesaver come aboard, but he sometimes floods the engine. Want to say here before I forget—the mind leaks like a sheet metal sieve—that if we take the project on, we may want to play with your title."

"He's right," Joe said to Jane. "It's overly optimistic."

"Not with God's help."

"You and God need to become reacquainted," Herk told Joe. He blew out a lungful of air.

"This isn't your book."

"Thank the Lord."

"Herk!"

Charlie suddenly twisted toward the door.

"Begging to interrupt." Candy, the art director, stood in the opening whose jamb Charlie had puttied last weekend. He'd gouged it with a paperweight thrown at Benji because the much younger man had started guffawing at his boss's rage over a glitch in Windows 7 that Charlie kept forgetting how to bypass.

"You wanted cover layout finished by two-thirty and I've got to get on it." Blonde hair cropped, Candy held up a title page reading, *You Done Good, Girl: How to Hopscotch into a Hopeful Relationship After You're Sixty*, by *Kittie Rehmeyer*.

"Well, fiddlesticks and bumblecock, get cracking," Charlie said.

"You asked me to wait."

"Why?"

"So you could decide between Helvetica and Cheltenham."

"Helvetica, of course, you know how I love the little nipples in the a's."

"I didn't know, actually."

"Now you do. I told Benji to inform you I'm in conference."

"I'm here on my own initiative, Charlie."

"Initiate an exit, will you?"

In saluting, Candy dropped the sheet of paper. She stooped for it. Her leather suede skirt billowed as she whirled and vanished. Clicks from her flats slapping the ancient floor grew fainter.

"Remind us children that patience wins over tantrums," Charlie said. He squared several-dozen query letters on his blotter. "If my daddy hadn't been Mississippi's top Ford-truck salesman—and if he hadn't died youngish and left me with a bundle to buy south-side rentals in our City Different here—I'd be long gone following the greyhounds or ponies and not confabbing with you good people, figuring how we can make a killing on as important a testament to rationalism as your book is. On the get-set and go, am I?"

In the dim light Joe, Jane, and Jane's son stared at him until Herk declared, "I might have chosen Clarendon."

"Clarendon?" Charlie asked.

"More panache."

"Panache? What the withers are you talking about?"

"A typeface with ascenders and descenders that say, 'This you don't put down, this you read.'"

"Never heard of it," Charlie said.

"I'll wager your art director has. Okay I go talk to her while you three gab?"

Charlie threw his palms out. "Far end of the hall's off limits."

Herk slumped against the couch's cushion, vowing to get to know her better.

"Benji! Jesus, boy, move along." Charlie shouted, as he scanned Jane's face, then Joe's. "If everyone did only as they chose, we'd have anarchy before Antarctica and Greenland and Tibet drop enough ice to raise the planet's oceans."

He grabbed the manuscript's top pages and read aloud, "*Lester Brown—whoever he is—and staff outlined the problems and solutions in their* Plan B: Mobilizing to Save Civilization. *We face extinction. But there is a way out to compel us to follow Lester's lead. Albert Schweitzer—him I know—the Nobel Peace Prize organist, and organizer of the hospital in Africa, though he adored Richard Wagner, discovered a universal ethical philosophy, Reverence for Life. By practicing this principle, and when we can't, by remembering the slogan of Al-Anon, AA's sister program, Detach with Love, accept others exactly as they are, we can continue producing the glories that justify the human race's presence.*

"Why read this book? It offers hands-on, easy-to-accomplish ways for changing deadly mind-sets. For those of you..."

Charlie looked up and yanked an earlobe. "Yes, yes, and yes. This may be the most influential manuscript ever showed up here. Look this contract over, hard-copy royalty of twenty-five percent, double that for e-books. We can't afford advances. If you want to give us a shot, I'll make this priority, out in three months."

"Not soon enough, given the menace." Jane stood and stepped forward to take the contract from Charlie.

"Our usual gestation period runs two years."

"Better look the paperwork over, Mom."

"Not your concern, huh?" Joe said.

A lean young man with granny glasses and a ponytail tied in green ribbon—its ends reading *draft dodger runaway*—entered bearing a tray holding four mugs of coffee, paper napkins, packets of sweetener, and a miniature pitcher of two-percent. "What a morning." His shorts and pocketless tee matched Charlie's. It had been the older man's brainstorm a year ago that they should dress like twins.

As Benji served the Tashes and Herk, Charlie said, "Mumbledee bandersnatch, Possum, you've been dawdling."

"Nope," Benji said without looking up. "First Vanessa calls to claim her astrologer nixes as bad karma the ISBN number for *Roses and Thorns* she asked you to select and show to her. Gonna retard sales. She also says friends are griping the book's going to be too thin, that you should have insisted on her writing thirty more poems."

He brought the tray to the front of Charlie's desk, balanced it with one hand while shoving aside a vase holding a spray of buffalo grass. He tore open two packets of stevia natural sweetener, poured in a dollop of milk, and offered it to Charlie.

"I said we'd get back to her and then Mad Dog called."

"What's he want?" Charlie asked.

"He's on his way over."

"He knows to make an appointment!"

"Claims *Big Howard Chisum and His House of Squaws* looks fine, loves your heirloom photo of guys dangling from a splintered branch, but that *a slice of history by Rolf Goodenough* has to be bolder and moved above the title. Plus he has changes on the galleys."

"And he pays for those."

"Told me to remind you he's our golden goose."

"You go phone his cell that I've raced on home with irritable bowel syndrome."

Benji turned toward Herk and the Tashes. "That's publishing, folks. Gotta be nuts to do what we do and we love it, right, Charlie?"

"Get your ass on the phone."

Benji started his retreat.

"Don't forget the tray."

Benji returned to snatch it up. He hurried into the hall.

"Coffee hot enough?" Charlie asked.

To Joe and Jane's nods Herk hunched his shoulders.

"The possum needs training. But turns out he's a whiz with figures. And a great bedside manner, as you saw. Keeps me in line. You wouldn't believe his story. I picked him out of Big Jo's Hardware three years ago—do a lot of my own repairs on this building and my spread in Las Campanas. Started seeking Benji out to help me find merchandise." Charlie poked his temple. "Quick and sharp. We got acquainted. Still smokes pot and brings his cat to work, but I pulled him off the vodka and into a 12-step program for fatties—a blubberhead, you wouldn't have known him—and got him to paying his alimony and child support. The wife, a real lush, had started knocking him around, calling him a fairy—lickety whompers, sired three children before he ran. The bitch wouldn't even let him kiss his own kids goodnight. Can you fathom the nutcase said she wanted *more*?"

He patted the manuscript. "I'm curious. How'd you get committed to this project? Not an easy book to write, I'd think."

"We—"

"I'll tell it, Jane." Joe turned to Charlie. "She always cries. Plus maybe I can condense what happened."

"Always gotta interrupt, don't you?" Herk said, gripping his thigh.

"Darling, please. Stay out of it?"

"I'll go take me a peek at the O'Keeffe. Museum's open Wednesdays?"

"Wouldn't know why not," Charlie said.

Herk emptied his mug, rose, bent to peck his mother's cheek. "Back in twenty minutes."

"Through a series of unexplainable coincidences," Joe began, "we, my wife and I, pinned our daughter, she was five, between Jane's back bumper and my front one, and Tatum, our sweet treasure, succumbed. Jane, stop." He lifted a hip and drew a handkerchief from the front pocket of his shorts and handed it to her.

"The aftermath proved devastating. So what that I'd just been promoted? We felt we could no longer call the East Coast home. Got discouraged, too, because we couldn't rev up enough enthusiasm for our proposed book from agents in New York that friends introduced us to."

"The Big Apple's a minefield," Charlie said.

"Jane's son had heard so much about Santa Fe from his wannabe-an-artist pals that the three of us decided to visit."

"And were captivated." She sniveled and blew.

"I can do my work for Goldman Sachs from just about anywhere. Herk lives on our property for now, does online whatever designing jobs he's scrounged. Six months ago we bought a house in Tesuque on the creek. Big lawn, which Jane had loved in New Canaan—here more a meadow, actually—and aspen scattered over the whole property."

"Wrigglety-piggety, yes and yes, everything makes sense except how did *You Can Save Us All* follow from the tragedy?"

"It," Jane managed before Joe broke in.

"Started because the marriage counselor we began seeing had read Lester Brown's *Plan B* and suggested we write a very needed, in her opinion, supplement, a kind of how-to guide. She felt that pouring ourselves into it might give us a new sense of purpose."

"And I believe God used her as His medium," Jane said. "Because, you see, she was right."

"Jane has her chapter on God and I have mine on techniques for organizing the world's billions. We got to talking with our neighbor in Tesuque, Marta Means—"

"One of our authors. A blessing to work with, as most of you, sorry to say, really aren't. If we could sell books composed by orangutans, my life and Possum's would be easier."

Joe glanced at Jane, who was now staring at the cedar-and-viga ceiling, handkerchief crumpled in her lap.

He said to Charlie, "Marta's enjoyed her experience with you a lot."

"Study the contract, call Benji for an appointment."

"If you're willing to speed up production," Joe said, "we're prepared to spend megabucks on promotion. Marta tells us that you don't bankroll—"

"Correct." Charlie spread his arms as though to semaphore. "Publicity's up to the author. We have our stomachs full creating product from a two-year backlog. And our Christian there will understand that God helps those who help themselves."

"We do have a budget," Jane said.

"That's what it takes." Charlie left his chair and stepped over a pile of southwestern nature books that, because the copyrights had expired, he planned to reprint, and hurried around the desk to shake Joe's and Jane's hands.

The front chimes sounded and the door slammed.

"Cockamamie hell. The wildfire that stopped three miles from Los Alamos I can cope with, even smoke fouling the golf course where I live. But the mad dogs have got me treed."

"Rolf," came Benji's voice. "Charlie's asked not to be disturbed. Give your changes to me."

The clacks of compressed-leather heels grew louder. "Hello, big guy, hello there, people."

The lanky, stooped newcomer stood clutching the ivory handles of a pair of .45s holstered on a belt scarred as though slashed. His furrowed nails were cracked, chipped, soiled, and half-an-inch long. He grinned under a tattered straw hat, coughed.

Why did Jane feel drawn to this scarecrow? The pistols? The ragged voice? The gingham shirt? The saddlebag looped over a shoulder?

"I can't talk with you now," Charlie said.

"Sure you can. These folks seem ready to depart. I'll cool my heels in the conference room. Sorry, ma'am, forgettin' my manners." Rolf removed his hat, dipped a chin as cleft as that of the dead movie hero, Kirk Douglas—and turned, so Jane thought, like a has-been ballet dancer.

"What kind of books does that particular mad dog write?" Joe asked when Rolf had left.

"Historical can't-say-if-they're-fiction-or-not. Swears not. Billy the Kid, Kit Carson, Pat Garrett, Doc Holliday stuff. I've been at this thirty years and the texts I see all blend in. Can't tell what's real anymore. Crazy world."

"No more than the world of shorts and longs," Joe said. "Let's go find Herk, leave this gentleman to his author."

"Thanks from the basement of Dante's *Inferno*," Charlie said.

Joe stood, took Jane's elbow.

Shaking it free, she asked Charlie, "Are we both followers of Jesus Christ? Thought I'd like to ask."

"Rolf's your main man for that. Matthew, Mark, Luke, John, and Tea Party Rolf. My dad was pure atheist and my mam a born-again Christian Scientist. Learned lots of useful stuff from her, though mostly you'd have to call me bipolar. Like the rest of us today, I suspect. I prefer bobbing around in my own bubble, pretend it's steel-clad, and try to turn out world-class books."

"Let's go, Jane."

Over her shoulder she thanked Charlie, then waved a little wave at Rolf. Boots on the table, he sat pushed back in a wicker chair beside the water cooler, gazing out of the conference room's doorway opposite Charlie's office.

A calico cat wandered into the hall, bell tinkling from a loop of red yarn. Jane stooped to scratch between its ears as Joe stepped into the heat and held the front door open for her.

After they'd gone, Charlie started cursing even before crossing the hall. "Gobbledygook and who's the crook, you son of a peckerhead. You think you can—"

"Surely do, Chas." Rolf swung legs clad in tapered chinos to the floor.

"You can't just barge in."

"Who makes you money like I do?" Rolf unbuckled his saddlebag, hauled galleys of his newest book out. "Got some wishbones to pick, pard. Hyphenations, woulds or coulds, semicolons looking to simplify into commas for impact, that sort of thing. Plus where *Rolf Goodenough* settles in on the cover."

"Benji!" Charlie shouted, then to Rolf, "Eleven cents a word at this stage for changes. I don't have to put up with this. You make your appointment like everyone else and we'll see what we see."

"Ever seen these freed?" Rolf leapt off the chair, whipped out the .45s, spun them once from the trigger guards, and from his hip pointed the left pistol at Charlie and the right pistol at Benji, who'd just appeared. "One of these maximizers is loaded. You boys care to guess which?"

2

Too Much Talk

In the news:

"Those trees just went whoosh," said stunned county sheriff Clyde Dennison. "The fire's still threatening you're-may-be-looking at 500 homes and businesses. It's the largest blaze in New Mexico history, with more to come closer to Arizona."

The Government Accounting Office predicts half of those near retirement age won't be able to cover expenses, including health care. Considering ever-lengthening life spans, the Social Security Deficit Commission urges increasing the retirement age to 70 to cut costs.

Nation-building in Afghanistan, after ten years of fighting Al-Qaida and the Taliban, bogs down amid tribal vendettas—this despite America's vast investment in equipping Afghan forces.

Joyce Chen becomes the youngest woman to win four LPGA majors. Of her idol, former Masters champ Lila Bottingham, Chen says, "We get together as often as we can to drink superior wine and have a little chat about what's going on."

That same day at three, after Jane's nap, Jane, Joe, and Herk gathered around the glass-topped table in the breakfast nook of the Tesuque hacienda the Tashes had purchased six months ago for a couple of million dollars. The manuscript of *You Can Save Us All* and the Surely You Jest contract sat next to a basket of papier-mâché Tuscan poppies. Mounted on a ponderosa beam, a ceiling fan whirled above them.

Herk lived on the two-plus acres of Bermuda and buffalo grass, shaded by groves of aspen, in a one-bedroom casita that backed onto Little Tesuque Creek. A slate path led from a too-big garage up slate steps to the five-bedroom main house.

The wind kept clicking the tip of a dead cottonwood branch against one of the windowpanes that looked out on a late-blooming bed of iris. A squirrel scampered up the trunk as light bounced from the mirror of the red Dodge 2500 RAM pickup Joe had traded his Z3 for. The laserlike sunbeam shattered against the tumbler of limeade Jane was lifting.

Sitting opposite his mother and stepdad, Herk faced the kitchen's cherry-stained island and Sub Zero refrigerator and freezer clad in oak. He sniffed and drew his head back as though to sneeze. "Mom, you smell smoke? Even after closing the windows? You'd think we were in Manhattan."

"Not so acrid, Herk, surely."

Barefoot, his right toe forced by a bunion over its long mate, Joe had changed from cargo shorts into poplin slacks and a hibiscus-strewn short-sleeve whose upper buttons he'd left free. "TV says the hot shots brought in from somewhere in the Midwest have left. Meaning the Pacheco Canyon Fire is eighty percent contained three miles north."

"Listen," Herk said, grabbing up the contract, knuckles knocking the basket of poppies aside, "I want more information on this joker. What's the name of his press about? And him and his assistant wearing duds that match?" Herk gulped from his bottle of Bud Light and glared at the cottonwood-pecked window. "Damn tree branch makes me nervous. Tap, tappity tap, tap tap."

"Charlie Small's a philosopher," Jane said. "And probably thinks of Benji as his son."

"Nah. Boy toy," Herk said. "No one but a gay man or nutso would use expressions like wrigglety piggety or fiddlesticks and bumblecock. But who cares, right?"

"You obviously do," Joe said. "Gay? Maybe. Nutso? As Charlie said, who isn't today? Even sacrosanct you."

"Back off, huh?"

"You two have got to stop!" Jane ran her fist down the twist of dark hair hanging over her blouse. "We received an enthusiastic bill of health from our neighbor. Charlie Small's quirks don't worry me. He wants to publish our book! Contract there doesn't worry me. What does worry me are these wildfires. Should we have bought this place, do you think, Joe?"

Her husband shrugged, threw out his hands, then bit off a strip of jerky. Chewing it was keeping him from starting up cigarettes again.

"Herk's right," Jane said, "it's smoky in here."

"We'll put together an escape kit. Okay?"

"I feel like I'm in Oz, Joe, despite the meadow you found for me and those white-and-violet iris that keep flowering, I'm at a loss how."

"Listen up," Joe said. His teeth tore off another piece of the mesquite-smoked snack. "Marge Marriage Counselor in Hartford urged us to move west and launch the manuscript ay es ay pee. To give us a reason to rise and shine. It's taken nine months but we now own this two-point-six-acre Shangri-La and, like you said, may have found a publisher. Without the agony of going through an agent."

"Dude," asked Herk, "are you truly making enough day-trading or whatever it is you do to keep up the mortgage *and* eventually promote your and Mom's book in the ways you claim you intend to? Goldman Sachs is in a jugular-cutting lawsuit, n'est pas? With the SEC for insider trading involving some East Indian board member? I know right now I'm leaning on your and Mom's financial generosity and I do appreciate it. Love wandering around here sketching, painting, having a beer at Tesuque Market or staring at the sculptures in Shidoni Park and watching sparks fly at the foundry."

"Not your business, Herk, how I'm making sufficient income. Got to peel myself off the computer, though, join a gym. Headaches worsening, back hurts like hell, and stomach cramps keep me from sleeping."

Jane startled. "This is true? Why aren't you seeing a doctor? Oh, I feel so isolated. You at your twin screens, Herk tramping the woods or whatever most days. It's so hard to make friends here. Even the parishioners at Holy Faith are more standoffish than at church back in New Canaan."

"About friends, I don't agree, Mom. Hey, lots of people here are open. Like that art director this morning."

"Herk, sweetie, you have a history. She was wearing a ring."

"So?"

"And by the way," Joe said to her, "you've also got a ring. I don't appreciate the way you eyeballed that Hopalong perp with the six-guns who barged into Charlie's office."

"Yeah, Mom," Herk said. "Whoever he's talking about."

"Oh, for goodness sake, stop it!" Jane mopped her eyes with a paper napkin and downed the rest of her limeade.

"We agreed to spend an hour brainstorming," Joe said, "and all we're doing—"

"Is bickering."

"Per usual," Herk said.

"Gimme that contract." Joe shot out his hand. "This *Grant of Rights to Publisher*, first paragraph. Must be forty lines long!"

"Should we take it to a lawyer?"

"Aah." He raced through the top page, turned it, scanned the second.

"Dude, too fast," said Herk.

Joe sipped from his glass of water, turned another page, another. "What's this? *Confidentiality. The parties agree not to disclose to any third party confidential information.* Like what? We'll ask. Also about electronic rights, also name of the press. Let's see that table of contents."

"You've read the whole contract, Joe?"

"Speed-reading's how I got to where I got at Goldman. Lester Brown agrees—*wartime* speed is what we need these days. Wind turbines and bullet trains in place worldwide by twenty-twenty? Impossible. Or maybe not, who knows?"

"Our book will help, won't it? Look, the puffball clouds are darkening." Jane stood, switched on the halogens embedded between ceiling beams. She swiped her eyes. "I'm sorry."

"For chrissake, you'll wet the paperwork. Tatum's gone, she's gone, Jane, kaput. It's been a year."

"Folks! Hola! Focus. Table of contents—I've told you before, you're operating in Never Never Land. Most of us are hardwired wrong to make the changes required to survive. But let's take another look." Herk fanned the typed sheets across the table:

You Can Save Us All

Applying Reverence for Life *and* Detach with Love *to stop the devastation*

Preface: Why Read This Book? Problems and Solutions Synopsized

Part I: Our Civilization's Situation

Part II: What You (and We) Can Do to Save Us All

Chapter 1: Doctor Albert Schweitzer and Al-Anon's Lois Wilson Lay It on the Line

Chapter 2: Easy-Does-It Disciplines to Change Destructive Mind-Sets

Chapter 3: Groups Build Leverage—a How-to Guide

Chapter 4: Closet Prayer, Prayer Circles, and Institutional Worship

Chapter 5: Finding or Creating Win-Win Work That Pays Top Dollar

Chapter 6: Let's Tend Our Gardens (Voltaire)

Chapter 7: Let's Beautify Our Homes, put the lie to Pascal's All human evil comes from mankind's inability to sit quietly in a room

Chapter 8: Dressing to Give Pleasure

Chapter 9: Cooking Our Way to Serenity

Chapter 10: No Time to Dither—Get Going!

Notes

Index

Acknowledgments

Contact the authors

"You actually believe all this?" Herk asked.

"You know the Lord can do anything with us He wants to, sweetie. And I believe He wants us to publish this book."

"Forget God," Joe said. "Look how Martin Luther King not only integrated the South but helped stop the mayhem in Vietnam. Before your time, Herk."

"Umm hmm. And someone shot King dead. Now we've got a Martin Luther look-alike mucking about in the White House, funding mayhem in Libya, Pakistan, Iraq, Afghanistan, and who knows where next?"

"It appears we'll get rain at last," Jane said, gazing through several of the window's twenty-four panes.

"What does that matter?"

"Rain matters, Joe. You two exhaust me. Or I exhaust myself. Let's discuss our title before I cave."

"*You Can Save Us All*. Why not *We Can Save Us All*?" Herk asked.

"Because it sounds redundant or that the *We* implies us, the coauthors, are tooting our own horns, rather than the *We* implying God and all the people."

"Actually," Joe told Herk, "I liked *We Can Save Mankind*, the lilt and all, God or not, but your mother called it sexist so I suggested *humankind* or *homo sapiens* or even *humanity* or *human species*. No soap."

"Those words sound stilted is why I balked. But Charlie seems to have doubts about *You Can Save Us All*. I guess *We Can Save Us All* is okay as an alternate."

"How about *We Can Save the Human Race*. Bit of rhyme there, too."

"What about *With God's Help We Can Right Our Planet's Wrongs*?"

"We the people might be able to," Joe said.

Jane groaned and pressed the sides of her head. *You Can Save Us All* or *We Can Save Us All*. That's it. Single-syllables. Lord, this babble." She'd thought to kiss Joe's neck but changed her mind. "I'm going to lie down."

"And I'll be back in a couple of hours." Herk rose and stretched.

"Where to?"

"Somewhere far from here."

"Want a bit of company?" Joe asked.

"No."

"Take an umbrella, please?"

"Those aren't rain clouds, Jane, they're smoke."

Herk bent to the floor for his mother's napkin, handed it across, then headed for the dining room and foyer.

When the front door had closed, Joe swung his arm around Jane's shoulder. "Babe? Let's try for another child. Want to? We might get lucky with twins."

She shrank away from him. "How can you joke? After the publicity we suffered through, the inquest, the lawyer's fees, the heart-wrenchings?"

"I'm not joking."

"I don't want another child! I want Tatum. And I want my mother."

"Gone, too, Jane."

"I need someone to hold. You and I? We're agents of Satan, Joe."

3

Come Hither

In the news:

An Al-Qaida informer in Yemen told government officials that surgically implanted explosive devices are being tested in terrorists to get past international-airport detectors. Beefed-up security measures will include more bomb-sniffing dogs and an increased use of swabs.

Los Alamos National Laboratory has put 10,000 running experiments on hold—including studies for extending the lives of 1960s-era nuclear warheads and attempts to improve the reliability of plutonium pits—until the 204-square-mile Los Conchas fire burns itself out.

Single mom tries to poison lodger with an antifreeze-laced blueberry smoothie after the 78-year-old widower slapped, then groped, the mom's 16-year-old daughter, who hasn't been able to speak a word since the incident.

Tonight at 8:00 on CBS, *Rules of Engagement* star Oliver Hudson (Adam) tries to figure out what's causing his eye to twitch until his cleaning lady shows up and solves the problem in an unexpected way. Expect, however, the usual antics from the show's two cats.

"If I could fuck this I would," Charlie Small told Benji the following evening. After dinner, Surely You Jest's assistant had loosened his hair, letting it flow to his shoulders. The two men sat sipping port under Charlie's back portal that looked out at flagstones surrounded by a pink-flowered, creeping thyme. At the courtyard's center sat a raised bed of the tubular, red-orange honeysuckle that Charlie's now-dead partner, Dr. Buck Monk, had planted to attract hummingbirds, grown scarcer as global warming nudged them north. Marigolds, three-trunk clumps of aspen, and apricot trees camouflaged a surrounding wall.

What Charlie wished to fuck was a gray-covered tome held against his belly entitled *Specimen Book and Catalog*, published in 1923 by the long-gone American Type Founders Company. It contained over a thousand yellowed pages showing typefaces like Cloister Cursive and Jenson Oldstyle, hundreds of decorative borders, and photos of feeders, cabinets, and presses.

The day's heat, less now but still over eighty degrees, wet a rectangle in the publisher's green knit where the book pressed. He watched the sinking half-sun light wisps of smoke above unseen Chicoma Mountain south of Los Alamos, then jerked the book onto the glass-topped table where his tumbler rested. "I used to have this behemoth book by heart. So that Paul Bunyan son of our maybe authors—from whom we heard nothing today, by the way—knows comparatively nada about typefaces. Even lovely Candace knows less."

Charlie watched Benji's hair billow as the younger man teased a reefer from the pocket of his own green knit, and lit the twisted end. He inhaled, aligned the lighter's corner with that of the bench, and blew out smoke with a flourish.

"I wish I could break you of that," Charlie said.

"Sorry, compadre—hot damn!"

Benji ducked as a dark shape swooped above him, veered, flitted back from the slider leading to Charlie's bedroom and out from under the portal's vigas to angle up over the apricots. Charlie and Buck had had eight of the trees planted after Buck purchased the four-bedroom, six-bath hacienda eleven years ago.

The airborne question mark darted and zigged faster than a swallow, hurtled down, tore past the honeysuckle centerpiece and, flapping veined wings, smashed into the slider and dropped into a Zuni pot from which the white trumpets of datura were unfolding to greet the evening.

The two men hurried close.

Black-marble eyes stared up as the leaflike ears quivered and a tiny jaw—clenched against needle teeth—opened and shut. The bat seemed to kneel, wings bent like Short Stuff's paws when she crouched. Benji pulled the marijuana cigarette from his lips. "It's got my cat's face, shaved, if you bashed in her nose. Let's bag and bury it. I can't stomach the suffering."

"Fiddlesticks and bumblecock. We'll leave it be a while."

"That's cruel, Charlie! Haven't you got a shovel or sledge? At least let me scoop it up."

"Allowing your emotions to rule again? Mary Baker Eddy—remember? Infinite *Mind*, Benji. Not emotions. And Mind's manifestations—you, me, the bat. Either its echo locator heals or the beast expires. But we don't interfere. Stay with me tonight?"

"Huh?" Benji drew from the reefer and distanced himself from the clay pot.

"Bring along your chair and that bottle. Let's give this weird-eared manifestation of Infinite Mind room to breathe."

Benji shuddered, followed Charlie to the far corner of the portal, where a carved door opened into the great room and its fountain.

"Will you stay? I get lonely."

"What happened to that woman near the clubhouse you could call, who'd tell her husband she'd forgotten to buy bananas for breakfast and needed time alone, anyway?" Benji blew more smoke, stubbed out the coal, twisted the reefer's end closed, and stuffed it into his pocket.

"She went into St. Vincent yesterday for a hysterectomy."

"Someday I might hang around, why not? Tonight I'm bushed."

"That letter this morning from Sotheby's big cheese shook me up, Possum."

"No emotions, bud."

"If we lose Sotheby's, Infinite Mind needs to find us a replacement soon. I'm paying a second mortgage."

"I know that."

"You inherit everything I've got, Possum."

"So you've said."

"Then stay."

"Short Stuff calls. And, begging your pardon, you shouldn't have bad-mouthed the Sotheby's cheese. I had to run down the hall to keep Candy company, that's how loud you got on the phone, yelling that his brokers were trailer trash, emptying their ashtrays in the parking lot, throwing Styrofoam cups into the chamisa or whatever—I never saw any cups in the chamisa, Charlie."

"I can't help my words when I get upset."

"What's worse than your rages? The silences. They numb Candy and me out."

"Probably worse on her—lickety-spittle, there goes our flying cat."

As though drunk, the bat zigzagged out from the datura and staggered, flapping, into the courtyard and over the wall. It beat the air above Benji's MINI Cooper parked on the cobblestones outside the garage that held Charlie's CLS-Class 402-horsepower Mercedes coupe, then swerved up to where they spotted it scooping a black hole through smoke the disappeared sun was coloring orange and lavender.

Charlie emptied his tumbler, poured more port, closed tired eyes, and after a moment said, "Silences? Holy Mary Baker, how I love them, especially since Buck went blue on me in oh four. We'd lived together for four years. Thought maybe I'd have better luck with women. But they hate silences, much prefer I'd rage. At least you put up with that."

The liver-spotted hand of the man Benji credited with saving his life descended on his wrist. He let it stay.

"Sooner or later you're gonna want to move over here. Jiminy crickets, look at this place, wine room, library. You could start out in the guest casita, even it has a hot tub. And Buck loved his golf. In his honor I've kept up Club membership. Clay-court tennis, horses, indoor lap pool, outdoor pool, weight room, seminars in the clubhouse. Life of Reilly, Benji, and an easy eleven-mile commute through countryside unmatched for its loveliness."

Charlie's palm had started to sweat. Benji slid his wrist from underneath it and took up his glass. "Only two miles to work for me now and when would I find time to play? I already put in twelve-hour days for you, eighty-four hour weeks."

"You're the heir."

"Of what, exactly? You've never had me sign any papers. Driving Sotheby's away was not a smooth move, bud."

"I own to that, Possum, okay? Life was easier at Surely You Jest inside the dot.com bubble. Buck was saving stroke victims at St. Vincent, we drank a bottle of Chateau Lafite every night, I was publishing fifty titles a year and clearing forty grand. Then I walked into our bathroom and, bless my garters, there's mister heart surgeon keeled off the toilet."

"You've told me, Charlie."

"And you're worried about not signing papers? Vacate that garage you inhabit and you'll see papers all righty-o, not to worry. We're going to make it through hard times with this manuscript of the Tashes."

"No phone call today, you said. What's *that* noise?"

The whirr grew louder. They watched a pair of hawk moths zoom toward the datura. They commandeered a couple of blossoms and, fluttering white-striped wings, began to drink.

"Benji boyo, you like critters. Out here we bring you wildlife twenty-four seven. You want another kitty cat? No problem."

How Benji wished he were home in his converted garage, that no letter from his mother had arrived, that he was propped in bed stroking Short Stuff, laughing at her eyebrows twitching, watching the Lady Gaga fund-raiser.

"What are your cover ideas?"

"Huh?"

"For the new manuscript. The cover, Benji, cover!"

"You don't have to shout."

"How 'bout this? A wraparound crowd of protesters, signs hoisted, slogans painted on them from chapter heads— against a backdrop of a deer drinking from the pool under a waterfall. On the back cover that same deer gutted, strapped to the top of my Mercedes."

"Sounds complex."

"Aah. You assemble a few buddies, I'll take photos, and Candy'll PhotoShop in the deer."

"I have no buddies, Charlie."

"Secret buddies? Buddies from Overeaters Anonymous?"

"You're the one who drummed it in when you gave me the job three years ago, who needs friends? You got your poison-pen letter from Sotheby's today and I received an epistle from my mother." He lifted his hip to extract the envelope. "You might as well know. She's looking to leave the Bay Area and settle in Taos."

"Don't joke, Possum."

Benji unfolded a blue sheet. "Direct from the horse's mouth. *Benjamin, I bear news. Since you refuse to see your children and have not come to see me since May of two-oh-oh-eight, I have decided it's a long-suffering beldam's privilege, duty, and right to see you. Therefore, I'm putting my condo up for sale and purchasing an earthship in Taos in which to end my time. Only three hundred and a few miles from Boulder and sixty miles from Santa Fe. To simplify your helping out when I start losing whatever marbles remain.*

"*I intend to continue writing verse and to visit Marian and the children. To visit you as well, Benjamin, four times a year as funds allow. In spite of everything I send love. Your mother.*"

Charlie leapt up and as he did, metal slamming into metal, followed by what seemed a sprinkle of glass, sounded outside the courtyard perhaps a football-field's distance away. Benji rose, too, but Charlie, driving a hand to Benji's shoulder, forced him back into the canvas-seated chair.

"Drunks out there. Not our concern."

"Nine-one-one, Charlie!"

"Foolio poontang, I'm already stressed to the max. They've got their smartphones or somebody has a cell." Charlie started swiping his hair, pacing back and forth along a bed of marigolds while the day's last bee rummaged in and out. "Your mother thinks she can invade our turf? Poof, done? Ball-breaker, minx, fishy old bag. I've told you what I laid on my own mam when she started bawling over the phone, knowing Buck and I were tight."

"You and I aren't—"

"Not yet. I want you to contact your genetrix and lay down you don't appreciate her upsetting the applecart."

"What applecart?"

"Stop playing possum with me."

They paused at the sound of a faraway siren.

"Even though Mam used to club my daddy's Adam's apple when he decided to beat on me," Charlie said, breaking the silence, "I told her I intended to make a relationship work with a man and that it *was* working, as it did not work with the Homecoming Queen at Old Miss I married, whom Mam excessively did love. And that she, Mam, should stay put and not come visit—thinking long-term to move out here—because the man I was living with, and learning to love, did not favor the fairer sex, except to try to save hearts on the operating room table."

The wail of the siren grew.

"Benji?"

"What?"

"C'mere, will you?"

"Time to head out, Charlie."

"I need some loving, Possum."

"Someday, maybe."

"Now." Charlie reached to grab the younger man's arm but Benji scooted away as the noise of the siren wound down and stopped. "C'mere!"

Benji began running, Charlie wheezing behind him, across the flags toward an arch in the wall, under a sky fast losing its radiance. He jiggled the gate's latch but it wouldn't lift.

Fingers gripped his elbow.

"Let me go!"

"I need help relaxing, Benji."

Charlie's protégé spun and slapped his cheek. "Back off, mister, or you won't see me tomorrow."

Charlie stood panting and staring a long while, palm cushioning the still-stinging flesh of his cheek. "I quit," he said at last. "That latch—gotta reset the gate. You'd better use the front door. Possum? What're we going to wear tomorrow?"

4

Coping

In the news:

Public Service of New Mexico (PNM) changes its mind, vows to fight the Public Regulation Commission's directive to buy more wind for its customers. PNM's CEO cites skyrocketing open-land prices and high maintenance costs for the giant turbines.

"If my caretaker had been there when the tree fell on the line, it would have been a small burn, not the start of New Mexico's largest wildfire," claims ranch owner Roger Cox. "Instead, it's an act of God. Who else would have directed Jim to search out the lost steer three miles distant?"

President Barack Obama warns of calamitous worldwide consequences if congressional leaders continue stonewalling his plea to increase by $4 trillion the government's borrowing limit, now capped at $14.3 trillion.

Dear Abby: After seven years of hiding from my first husband when he came home soused, I thought my second husband was going to be perfect. Then he moved in. He became distant and moody and spent most of the day in front of the TV.

Short Stuff sat mewing in her carrier as Benji downshifted his bumble-bee-colored MINI Cooper to manage the turn onto Chappelle. The whine of the stalled air conditioner after his two-mile commute — worsened by Short Stuff's plaints — was making the back of his head throb.

Following the call from Jane Tash on Friday to set up a signing appointment for today, Monday, at 9:30, last night Charlie had called Benji to discuss appropriate garb. Though the younger man wore the short-sleeved button-down, khaki shorts, and leather sandals that Charlie had bought them at the Discount Center in May, the undersides of Benji's thighs already were sticking to the Cooper's black leatherette. Santa Fe faced a mid-afternoon high of ninety-one degrees.

There stood Charlie's black Mercedes—fourteen speakers and a rear-view camcorder that snapped into action every time the publisher shifted into reverse. He'd traded Buck's two-door Mercedes coupe, which Charlie had waxed every Sunday, for this twin-turboed brute just a month before lashing out at Sotheby's managing director.

In front of the *For Lease* sign on the corner of the Surely You Jest building rested Seymour Sabatini's white Corvette. Charlie hadn't told Benji that the latter-day poet and philanthropist—earlier a commercial real estate broker in Chicago—had called to squeeze in time before the Tash couple's arrival.

Benji braked for a homeless couple. She sat in a wheelchair, a lidded pot weighing down her smock. The man pushed her in sockless high-tops, bedrolls strapped beneath his pack, sleeping bags reaching above his head. After they'd crossed toward the El Dorado Hotel, Benji parked next to art director Candy Carlton's Miata convertible.

Short Stuff stopped whining as Benji gripped the handle of her carrier and swung her out. Whiskers and eyebrows stuck through the mesh she pressed her nose to. Hopeful that Charlie and Seymour were locked in talk so that Benji could dodge a raking over for appearing five minutes late—or, more unsettling, a drawn-out silence—he passed the three apricots spreading greenery along the windows of the front office and conference room. On turning the corner, he picked a half-empty Bud Light from the gutter, and pulled open the front door.

He tucked the beer bottle in his armpit to grab up the stack of mail. He emptied his lungs in relief. Sir Publisher sounded busy in his own office delivering one of his author put-downs. Benji ducked left, hid the bottle in the wastebasket, set the carrier on a chair, unzipped the flap, and took envelopes and packets to his desk.

A minute later he'd refreshed Short Stuff's bowl of water and high-end kibbles from the sack in the closet, and topped off the litter in her polypropylene box.

Across the hall, wearing the same outfit as Benji, Charlie took a sip of coffee cooled by two-percent milk and sweetened by stevia, then slowly rose behind a desk twice as large as Benji's. "You," he said to the multimillionaire seated in front of the wall holding two-hundred Surely You Jest titles, "are a far-too-crappy, sentimental poet to stomach, verbose beyond ten cunts gabbing, creator of cesspools exhausting to edit—and a Surely You Jest original whose work, such as this latest collection of sonnets and villanelles"—Charlie hoisted past his shoulder a green binder that had lain beside the *Britannicas*, and waved it like a flag—"contains must-publish, must-read treasures that in my opinion, and I believe Benji's, will outlast most of the other sweated-over, finely produced products of this press."

"Shot your wad, oh mighty Pooh-bah?" Seymour Sabatini, even more carefully groomed than Charlie, rubbed his hands together. A woman whose apartment he paid for, in exchange for overnight favors, trimmed his nails twice a month. Their ten crescent moons gleamed under the floor lamp that Charlie, having as usual arrived at seven, had switched on.

"Have I signed off? Not quite, my head-in-clouds, feet-of-clay poet and cherished hack."

"Then what?" Sabatini smoothed his mustache, two patches bristling a pencil-line lip.

"Our lessee has flown the coop."

"Sotheby's," Seymour said.

"Squeezing our cash flow."

"I'll find you someone."

"Let us hope. Because Surely You Jest wants to publish this"—Charlie slapped the green binder—"perhaps your finest collection, though frankly I know little about poetic craft."

"No need to know. Do need to publish. Gives me points with the ladies." Seymour pinched up the thighs of Levis slimmed at the ankles, revealing silk socks above alligator shoes. "Pockets enhanced by my Pakistani widow at White Cloud Silver-and Turquoise on Marcy." Each one displayed a dollar sign enclosed in an embroidered squash blossom.

Charlie glanced at the stubby clock his grandfather had assembled from waterworks' parts and set in a walnut case. The Tashes were due any moment. Had Benji arrived? Again last night the boyo had refused to stay over.

"Rub-a-dub," the publisher said aloud.

"That's as strange a response as the name you've given this outfit. Where'd you come up with it, anyway?"

Charlie squinted at him a long time.

"What's the matter?"

"Later."

"You want me to find you a tenant?"

Charlie scratched a spider bite on the side of his neck. "When light trucks from Japan seriously started eating into Ford sales, my daddy, Mississippi's leading dealer, clamped a butcher knife between a couple of concrete blocks, and pitched onto it. My uncle and I found him in the garage. We were heading out for a Sunday afternoon bird hunt. When we saw Daddy's face hanging over that mess of blood, Uncle Allen said, 'Surely you jest, Nate."

"You putting me on?"

"You need to shoo. I've got a couple of deep pockets coming in to sign a contract."

The little man with the double mustache leaned toward him. "First tell me what's next with my manuscript."

"You've already done one book with us. Go to your *Author's Guide*, prepare the text file for e-mail. Not *in* the e-mail. As an attachment."

Charlie thought he heard the front door chimes ring. He wiped his forehead.

Benji appeared, cradling Short Stuff. "The Tashes are here. Marta Means came with them."

"At least they had the sense not to bring her son." Charlie's voice rose. "What are you doing holding that shabby tabby?" He thrust the green binder at Seymour. "Returned to you. Cats soften the boy's brains.

"Get the feline back where she belongs," he told Benji, "and heat the coffee."

"Seymour, we all set? Deely dooly, I love you truly. Find us cash flow, bro," Charlie's eyes found the next target. "Welcome, Tashes."

Seymour rose as Joe, Jane, and their Tesuque neighbor walked in behind Benji. "The Tashes and Marta." He settled his granny glasses and turned.

"Candy would appreciate a cup of your java, too," Charlie called out to Benji. "Seymour, two of these people are new to Surely You Jest. That manuscript Jane Tash is carrying may transform America from a nation of lemmings to a nation of pit bulls. You've met Marta Means? Writing memories of childhood for us."

"Haven't had the pleasure." Before even noticing her long nose, Seymour watched the breasts of the tanned woman in riding boots and jodhpurs smooth wrinkles from the blouse she wore beneath an open vest. He relished its scent of leather. "Sonnets and villanelles are my beat," he said, rising. "Though time's coming to think about a memoir myself."

When he'd left, Charlie threw his arm in an arc and invited the remaining authors to sit.

"Marta, our Tesuque neighbor, is joining us for emotional support," Jane said, dressed for the day's heat in a sleeveless sundress. "Since she's worked with you, we thought maybe she could ask questions Joe and Herk and I didn't write down."

Marta swung a tooled boot onto the opposite knee. "Happy to oblige," she said. Her rasp was that of a three-pack-a-day smoker, though she'd stopped cold six years ago after finishing her PhD.

"Let's get this ball rolling, okay?" Joe removed the straw hat he'd bought Saturday after deciding he wanted the *you-bet-I'm-a-stud* look of his stepson, Herk. He placed it on top of the briefcase covering his khakis, then reached to hang it on a post of the spindle chair, unsnapped his briefcase's lid, and extracted a Baggie stuffed with jerky. "Tackle the contract first?" Joe's jaw cracked as he started chewing.

"Can't you leave that alone till we're through?" Jane asked.

"Nope; I can't." He chomped the wad until it softened enough to swallow. "Charlie, Jane and I agreed this weekend that our son, Herk, needs to be part of the *You Can Save Us All* team. He wanted to be here but wrenched his knee this morning and said he'd better stay put with an ice pack."

"That's not exactly what he said, Joe."

Marta, who'd not met Herk yet, swung her black curls as though watching a tennis match, instead of Jane and Joe.

"Close enough, aren't I?" Joe asked. A sliver of jerky had refused to go down. He clutched his Adam's apple, squeezed, narrowed his eyes, gulped. "Talk, talk, talk. Like one of Goldman's Monday morning gather-rounds, figuring how best to diddle clients—let's get to the book contract. First question..."

Herk had lied about his knee. Having trailed Joe's Dodge RAM by ten minutes, he was now balancing on the hood of his own smaller pickup, wedged between two Russian olives screening Candy's mini-courtyard from the lot used by Sotheby's brokers and clients.

He'd hooked a leg over the wall's scabbed top when a grasshopper whirred off. His Stetson flew into the courtyard and he scrambled after it. On the way down his heel knocked a half-filled can of Pepsi from Candy's wire-mesh table, sending it clanging against one of her planter barrels. She glanced up from her screen and clapped a hand to her mouth.

In black shirt and denim shorts secured by a silver-buckled belt, Herk righted himself from the bricks and pushed a forefinger to his lips. His left knee stung. Sweat built in its creases as he watched blood drip along the shin into his sneaker. Wincing, he retrieved his hat, managed to rise, and limped between planters toward the slider.

Candy stared from her swivel chair while he slid the glass door back.

What a good-looking woman she'd stayed, older than him by what? Ten years? She'd dyed blonde the hair cropped an inch from her scalp? In the silence punctuated by the processor's hum, he mouthed the word, "Hi," and shook his shoulders as if to refit their expanse into his tee.

Candy rose, spun in miniskirt and pink-sequined shirt, strode to the hallway and buzz of talk from its other end, and shut her door. "You're bleeding!" She hurried close, wrested away the handkerchief he'd produced, and, squatting, blotted his knee. "We've got Band-Aids and peroxide in the conference room. Don't leave."

Herk clamped his palm to his heart to calm it, lowered himself to a bench on which she'd painted the faces of a jaguar, pack rat, badger, and antelope.

The sixty seconds she was gone seemed a mere two. She knelt again, wiped blood off with a hot washcloth, upended the bottle of peroxide to the cloth's other side, patted the wound, set disinfectant and cloth behind her, and pulled a Band-Aid from a shirt pocket.

She looked up—eyes the color of a tide pool Herk used to gaze into at the Coney Island aquarium—and handed him the dressing. Her hand shook. "What's your name again?"

"Herk. For Hercules." He peeled the wrappings off the bandage, pressed its ends to his skin.

"What's this about? Why over the wall?" She stood and smoothed her skirt, backed away until the workstation stopped her. Her wedding ring glinted under the ceiling's fluorescents. "What gives with you, Hercules? Hercules. Oh, my."

"I wanted to talk with you about the cover for my mother's and step-dad's manuscript. They and a neighbor are in your boss's office right now."

"If Charlie knew that you—you've never heard him rage."

"So let's talk quick and I'll do a Zorro over the wall. If you'll steady the table."

"Hilarious. What's the book called?"

"*You Can Save Us All.* Mom and Joe, and I guess your boss, think it can change enough mind-sets to stop the Republicans' blinders-on drive to install a Mitt Romney or Rick Perry or Herman Cain in the White House. Especially if the book's heavily promoted, which Mom and Joe say they can't wait to do. They have the funds, at least they claim to."

"So what are your ideas?" Candy eased her way around processor and printer and sat, planting her clogs on an abstract-expressionistic square of rug.

"Put me on the cover, head and hat." He shifted the Stetson to a thirty-degree slant and winked. "Kidding. The book's based on Albert Schweitzer's *Reverence for Life* and the founder of Al-Anon's *Detach with Love.* Fill the cover with head shots of them."

"I know all about Al-Anon. I have a Wednesday noon home group. My husband's, I'll be straight with you, a drunk."

"So's my dad."

Candy cast a thumb backward. "In there with Charlie and your mom?"

"Joe's my stepdad. My blood dad manages the Boston Hilton, last I heard."

"The problem is," Candy said, "that Al-Anon headquarters would never allow Lois Wilson on the cover of non-conference-approved literature."

"How do you know?"

"I just do."

"Show the back of Lois's head and just Albert's face full on?"

"Very funny. You'd better beat it, Hercules."

He jerked his shirt from his shorts.

"What are you doing!"

"Let's brainstorm." He drew out three yellow, ink-filled sheets that he'd tucked beneath his belt. "Table of contents."

"We're taking too big a risk."

"Charlie Small doesn't scare me."

"You don't have a job to lose."

"What's your husband do?"

"Child psychiatrist."

Herk glanced where she pointed. On a side table, chrome framed a fat man's head under a billed cap whose front read, *Babies Rarely Grow Up.* Sideburns reached his jaw. A plaque proclaiming *2010 New Mexico Book Awards* and Candy's name leaned nearby.

"I'm betting his line of work means you don't need a job. Ten minutes? To work out a cover that'll make this mother fly off the shelves?"

Candy stooped to retrieve a clock from a pile of PhotoShop and InDesign manuals lying on the workstation's lowest shelf, shoved it at Herk, pulled it back, placed it on top of the processor, and curled her fingers for him to come close.

"If we're interrupted, keep this." He bent to pluck a scrap of paper from her wastebasket.

"This what?"

He finished scribbling his cell number and handed the scrap to her.

Off the hallway's opposite end, Charlie wheeled his five-legged chair to the side of his desk. "Whoopedee-do-dah on the cover idea you just shared," he told Jane, "and I'm going to propose another. I own a big car, you saw it outside, I wax it every weekend, big Mercedes, frightening sight.

"Suppose for our cover we stage a gang of protesters hoisting signs lettered with your book's chapter heads. A gutted deer lies strapped to my bomber—zero to sixty in five-point-two seconds, by the way. If we flip to our back cover, we see that same deer above the blurbs you'll need to get, drinking from the base of a waterfall. The before of a beautiful creature as the good Lord made her and the afterward disemboweled atop a gas guzzler, black as our race's future if readers don't take to your manuscript's tips for salvation and turn them into mass movements fast."

From his hip pocket Charlie unfolded a hankie and mopped sweat from the back of his neck.

"But *You Can Save Us All* is meant to offer hope," Jane said.

"That's our point," Joe said. "A dead animal on top of a Mercedes makes me want to stop eating and drinking permanently, which I sometimes feel like doing anyhow."

"Oh, Joe, the state of your emotional health is *not* the point. I like my idea better, Mr. Small. Six, a dozen women, men, children—"she swiped her eyes with a knuckle—"dressed in their Sunday best, all ages, stare out at the reader, with the book's title and *Reverence for Life* and *Detach with Love* smaller below, then Joe's and my names, then—yes—somewhere the words, *A how-to book of survival.*"

"Folks, I'm lost." Marta raised an ankle to her thigh and began brushing invisible dust from the upper half of her boot.

"How can you cram all that onto a book cover?" Joe asked.

Charlie slammed down the *Britannica* topping his slush pile. "Squat diddily, people, are we here to sign a contract?" He drew a sheaf of printed sheets from a drawer and flourished them. "Our art director can sketch out a few cover mock-ups in minutes, small potatoes, no problemo. Yes? Dandy? What is it, Benji?"

All looked toward the door.

The man half Charlie's age removed his glasses. "Vanessa. In crisis mode again. I'll cut her off if you tell me to."

Charlie grabbed up his receiver. "Christ in the barn, I'm with authors, Vanessa. What's the matter?"

Joe blew his nose and Marta pulled an engagement calendar from her tummy purse while Charlie listened.

"Say a prayer, girl. You just successfully delayed publication of *Roses and Thorns* by three months." He clacked back the receiver and gazed at his guests. "Poets! Trying to broaden our list with them, but this babe... Asked could we hurry up changing her ISBN number so she can have copies to sign after reading at her fifteenth high school reunion. Library of Congress won't let you change an ISBN once it's registered. The woman's bonkers, don't get me started."

Marta looked up, knitting her eyebrows until they became one. "Shouldn't the Tashes think soon about scheduling readings?"

"You betcha, yes, ma'am. Start with Trevor-the-Fag down the street. Words, Words, Words Bookstore. Benji, why are you standing there? I need a heat-up and these folks need freshening. Take Candy a hit, too." Charlie thrust his mug toward him. "Vamoose, boyo."

He faced the Tashes. "Let's go over this agreement together quickly. Scoot those chairs closer."

They were discussing the *Confidentiality* paragraph on the last page when Benji called, "Knock, knock," and brought forward a tray of steaming mugs. He set them on the desk beside Charlie's vase of buffalo grass, left the tray of sweeteners and small pitcher of milk, and picked up a mug painted with a red pronghorn bucking. "For Candy."

Charlie uncapped his father's pen and scrawled his own name and the date. He turned the stapled sheaf around. As he handed the pen to Joe, a scream flew down the hall.

Charlie leapt from his chair, followed by Joe, who'd grabbed the jerky from his briefcase. They ran toward Candy's office. Benji stood transfixed inside, gripping a packet of stevia by its corner. Red shards and the mug's handle lay scattered across the art director's throw rugs. Coffee browned her white skirt and splotched her shirt a midnight blue, on which the pockets' sequins glittered like stars. Herk had straightened from his crouch behind the bench, his left hand gripped the slider's handle.

"What the fuck?" Joe yanked out a strip of jerky and bit it in two.

"I thought she was alone," Benji said. "I tripped."

"C'mere, you," Charlie said. "Not *you*."

Candy had stepped toward him from beside her workstation.

A motorcycle or mufferless low rider roared out of Sotheby's parking lot.

"What in the world of treachery have you—*c'mere*, I said—stored in that New York City mind that drove you to crawl in like a sun-struck peccary when I told you last week this woman *was* busy, *is* busy, is *always* busy producing typography and covers for authors who matter? C'mere, you pathetic hunk of pork."

Knuckles digging into his hips, Charlie began wheezing while Joe chomped his half strip of mesquite-cured beef.

Herk stopped at the workstation, using it as a barrier, and peered over Candy's monitor. "I thought—"

"I don't have time to deal with scumbag duplicity. Get out and take your east-coast kin with you." Charlie backed into the hall, yanking Benji by the elbow. He curved his hand past his shoulder. "C'mon, out. Out. Out the front door. You, too," he said to Joe and clamped his upper arm.

Joe wrenched himself free. "Speed it up, Herk."

Before Jane's son, tongue circling his lips, could reach the doorway, Marta Means came striding past conference room, mail room/mini warehouse, and john. Jane followed, stroking her twist of hair as though polishing it.

"Charles, Charles, whoa. Easy there."

His class ring bit into the neighboring finger as he let Marta squeeze his hands. He realized how top-heavy her breasts made her look.

"Eyes off the boobs, Charles. Not good for the old pump. What's happening here?"

"Candy let this lowlife divert her from her work and coffee has ruined her outfit. Good job, Possum, good aim with the coffee."

"I didn't aim, Charlie."

"Who is this guy?" Marta asked.

"My son," Jane said, standing behind her.

"We were talking cover ideas, Mom." Black-and-white sneakers squeaking, Herk sidled past his stepfather and Charlie into the hall. Marta kept her grip on the publisher's hands.

"Benji, sweep these people out of the building."

"Charles," Marta said, "perhaps this guy meant nothing wrong."

"He deceived me!"

"Maybe he just wanted to help."

"Bushwhack and bandersnatch."

Joe swallowed the rest of his jerky. "I'm not sure this is the right press for Jane and me. Surely You Jest? Though friends do say self-publishing takes too much grunt work. Plus zip cachet."

"Count me out either way," Herk said to no one.

"Of course Charles's is the right press for you," Marta said. "The name's memorable. You'll end up with an outstanding package. Charles? Bygones be bygones?"

"If this pork chop backs his lard ass out."

"I beg your pardon?" Jane said. "That's my son you're talking to."

"Forget it, Mom." Herk passed the others and strode on down the hall. He opened the front door but hesitated in the glare.

Benji stayed behind to help Candy clean up while Marta let Charlie lead her, Jane, and Joe back into his office.

"So it's yes?" Charlie pushed his chair to its regular spot behind the *Britannicas* and stack of queries.

"I guess," Joe said.

"I'm afraid you're all we've got," Jane said.

Marta kept her mouth shut, feeling a growing attraction to this transplant from New Canaan.

Charlie scribbled his name and the date at the bottom of page four, pushed contract and pen to the edge of the desk. The Tashes rose and signed.

"Watch who you're shoving!" came Herk's voice from the building's entryway.

"Late for appointment, pard."

Charlie jumped up. "Benji!"

Seconds later, the ponytailed office manager appeared. "Mad Dog's here, Charlie. Herk was just leaving."

"Call the cops."

"Rolf did make a date for this morning—did so last week, after you laid into him. I forgot to note it on a Post-it."

"Willies and a pox upon, can't you see Marta and the Tashes are still conferring here?" Charlie clamped his temples, mussing the sienna-dyed hair. He glanced at his clock. "Only eleven? I'm too old for this."

Joe pulled down his straw hat. "Let's make tracks." He clamped an arm around his wife's shoulder.

"Let me go, please."

"Possum, arrange to bring the Tashes back next week, mid-to-late. We'll need Candy, too. I promised to rush this project through and damned if I'm not going to do my damnedest to do it."

"Howdy again." Rolf Goodenough peered past Benji into the room. A bronze ring enclosing a five-pointed star and the words *United States Marshal* glinted from his pocket's flap. He reached up to vise the door's jamb. Jane noticed again how chipped his nails were. Feral, she thought, and felt her heart speed.

Herk had vanished. Benji led Joe and Marta into his office, but Jane held back. Dizzied by Rolf's sweet stench of tobacco, she threw her hand toward Charlie's doorway. "Mr. Small tells us you're a friend of Mark and Jenny."

"Tea Party Patriot? Sure am that, ma'am, yes, ma'am. You?"

Jane nodded.

"Corresponded with Mark Meckler and Jenny Beth Martin since they lit the first Tea Party bonfire in oh-nine."

5

Mix & Match

In the news:

Cornell University study shows that students nationwide are taking more, not less, time to graduate, due to deep cuts in public higher-education budgets, enrollment increases, and steep hikes in tuition. The longer students find they must take to finish, the more likely they'll drop out.

On Monday, negotiators again failed to agree on how to restart Palestinian-Israeli peace talks, dealing a blow to Palestinian efforts to become recognized by the UN as an independent nation. Skirmishes in the Gaza Strip and on the West Bank continue unabated.

With nearly half of July gone, year-to-date precipitation in Santa Fe has reached 1.33", a mere 21% of the Weather Bureau's official year-to-date norm. Bureau officials predict ongoing draught until at least November.

7-foot-6 NBA center Yao Ming expects to retire after nine seasons because of foot and leg injuries. "What's the point of watching now?" asks Lubingxia, online user of Sina Weibo, a Chinese Twitter-like site.

Late the next afternoon, hail bounced off the raised top of Seymour Sabatini's white Corvette, parked in the Words, Words, Words lot three blocks southeast of Charlie Small's building.

Inside the bookstore, with hail outside pounding the arched panes above him, Seymour bent over the copy of Donne's holy sonnets he was considering buying. The last of his croissant lay on a side table on a paper plate, next to a mug of now-tepid black tea. In plaid shorts, sandals, and a Ralph Lauren polo, the former real-estate developer perched on one of two armless sofas that faced each other, white muslin draping both.

A coffee table fashioned from mesquite and laden with *New York Times'* best sellers separated the sofas. The ceiling's black acoustical tiles muffled talk at the front register, behind which a sign from the *Santa Fe Reporter* proclaimed Words, Words, Words *Best of Santa Fe—2011 1st Place Winner.* In a back corner of the store stood the platform for readings. On its two encompassing walls—one orange, the other green—hung head shots of local writers and a massive bulletin board.

The conditioned air smelled of the monsoon season's rain that patrons had tramped in, plus coffee from pots brewing at the snack bar. Ceiling canisters highlighted the sofas, the islands of children's books, the cluster of greeting-card spinners, and a splayed Webster's *Third New International* lying on a rostrum.

"Hello, pussycat."

Seymour reached for his mug and peered up over half-moon reading glasses.

The bookstore's longtime owner, Trevor Quesenberry, stood with hands on hips, white loafers apart. He wore his usual linen slacks and matching cream-colored blouse colored by a blue neckerchief, sleeves rolled to the elbows. Gray hair, parted down the middle, covered his ears. His oversize nostrils flared as he asked, "Just when do you plan to get rid of that twinnish, half-assed mustache, O ladies' man?"

Seymour pushed his glasses to the top of his head. "When tickling no longer turns my favorite lady on."

"Doubt the mustache would do it for me, darling." Trevor shrugged. "Though who knows? Shall we find out this evening?"

Seymour burst into a belly laugh. "In spite of the e-book craze, no wonder this store is so successful. You never give up."

"Not till you say you're mine."

"Your canned come-on?"

"I have others. You buying today?"

"I think." Seymour closed the *Donne* so that Trevor could see the cover.

"When's your own next masterwork due? We should set up a reading."

Seymour threw out his hands. "Charlie's lousy at proofing. I'll need a couple of weeks to eyeball the galleys of *Babes in the Woods,* my new sequence of sonnets and villanelles. Yesterday I promised to find him another lessee—Sotheby's is moving out, probably due to one of his nib's tirades. So I'll be pushing for early publication. You want me to read, no hits?"

"I'll restrain myself."

"I'm serious, Trevor."

The store's owner bowed from the waist, fingers steepled.

Seymour extracted his iPhone and thumbed the calendar app. "Saturday, October twenty-two, say six o'clock?"

Trevor pulled a notepad from his pocket and uncapped a golden fountain pen. "If we're booked, I'll let you know. Otherwise, it's a date. What's your number?"

Seymour gave it, stuffed the last of the croissant past his mustache, and snatched up the *Donne*—because Marta Means had just pushed through from the vestibule. "Trevor, thanks!" Seymour sprang from the sofa, skirted the wicker chairs where a woman read to twins in pigtails, and aimed for the French doors.

Marta raised a hand, either in greeting or to indicate Whoa, slow down.

"Hi, there," Seymour called. Marta had traded yesterday's jodhpurs and riding boots for black leather shorts belted in silver, cockleshell conchos, and black high-tops. But it was the scoop-necked yellow knit that riveted his gaze. "The cloudburst—cooler outside?"

"Not much. Excuse, please?"

She strode past, her swish more that of a twenties-something hooker than of the post-menopausal, fifty-year-old Seymour supposed her to be.

She wheeled beside a rack bulging with tour guides and maps. "I'm sorry," she called to him, "you don't deserve my rudeness. A buyer's showing up to look at the gelding I'm selling off and I wanted to find a couple of Amazon best-memoirs-of-the-month before heading back to Tesuque. Help me choose?"

Seymour caught up and they moved toward the *Creative Nonfiction* placard chained to the ceiling near the public reading platform. He brushed one half-mustache with his middle finger as she ran her palm across the spines of a row of hardcovers and picked out *Love at Hindsight*. Her long nose twitched as though on scent.

"What did Charlie say you're working on now?" Seymour asked.

"My current effort's a flashback to the preteen years. I'm attempting to shape it into heroic couplets—honoring Alexander Pope—because those years were so special for me, so musical compared with the more-recent years I've been struggling to discover my sexual preferences. A painful time while earning the PhD." She freed a softcover tome called *Memories from the Womb*, by a male author, and faced Seymour.

"What's your doctorate in?" he asked, unable to keep from glancing at her cleavage.

"Anthropology from UNM. Just a few years ago, actually. I titled my thesis, *What the Skulls of Sixteenth-Century Zuni Women Can Reveal about Their Preoccupations*."

"I see. Can I buy you lunch tomorrow? I'm thinking about a memoir myself. Like to pick your brains."

"Pick me up, you mean?" She wagged her black curls, held by a band the same yellow as her knit. "Been there, done that. What is it with you guys, the bigger the tits the weirder you get. Charles turns bright scarlet."

"Just talking lunch." Look how you've dressed, lady, he felt like saying.

"No can do." Marta extended her left hand and Seymour took it. Cold.

He watched her retreat toward Trevor at the register, buttocks no longer bobbing. He trudged over to the placard lettered *Poetry* and found five copies of his first Surely You Jest collection, *Mayor Daley, Bye-Bye*, its cover a photo of the Sears Tower mantled in snow. He pulled a copy free, decided to call his Pakistani widow at work, ask her to fix lamb kebab and salad for two. He'd bring six roses, stay the night.

When he took his and Donne's poems back to the sofa, he saw that a stranger had filled his favorite spot next to the side table bearing paper plate and not-yet-drained mug. She'd set her elbows on a second table, separating the sofas, and dropped her chin to her fists.

He sat opposite, lay his books down, and lifted his tea.

"One of those books looks like a product of my publisher's," the young woman said, staring across. In contrast to Marta's rasp, the voice seemed honeyed. She was dressed differently, too: espadrilles topped by yarn bunched into blossoms, a filmy dress imprinted with hummingbirds—hem clinging to her calves—and a wide-brimmed, red-beribboned hat. "I'm Vanessa Z. Nord, one of Surely You Jest's poets, and my heart leaps whenever I see someone with a Surely You Jest title, even if it's not one of mine, though of course I wish it were. This store is my cradle and blankie. Not to lie, I'm here feeling sorry for myself. How about you?" Masses of auburn hair streamed down her back. A couple of sheaves dropped past dimpled cheeks and undulated to her ribs. A mole stood above a heavy left brow.

"I'm feeling sorry for myself, too."

"So why?"

"I'm a Charlie Small poet like you." He held up *Mayor Daly, Bye-Bye.* "Just set a reading date here for this."

"What a cute little mustache. Of course you're a poet, what else could you be? Not some old banker who's fleeced too many sheep and turned to verse for solace. Donne's sonnets—do you write sonnets?"

"And villanelles. How about you?"

"Oh, no, too restrictive, my poetry's hard to stop. My friends say my latest collection should have been twice as long. Partly that's why I'm pouting. Also because the ISBN number is *wrong*. But mostly because Charlie Small got mad at me on the phone yesterday and threatened to—"

"Vanessa, dear heart?" Trevor Quesenberry had swept close. The bottom of one leg of his slacks wrapped the foot of the coffee table. "You'll have to talk softer—until your reading. Before Thanksgiving, isn't it? I'm trying to keep a librarylike ambiance here. May I bring you an espresso?"

Vanessa shook her head. After he left, she rose and walked over to sit beside Seymour. "Do you mind? So we can talk without Trevor the Troll pouncing?"

"Not at all." Especially he liked the perfume she wore. Mimosa? The imagined aroma of his Pakistani's lamb kebob now sickened him. "So Charlie threatened you?"

"He did." Vanessa looked not at Seymour but toward the colored walls displaying the bulletin board and photos of authors. "I asked yesterday if he could hurry the production of my new book a wee bit so I could sell copies at my high-school reunion. He told me that, because I'd asked, he was delaying publication three months." She turned to Seymour and snuffled. "I'm looking for another publisher. There's a husband/wife team up on Tano doing a collection out of their mansion for my best friend. Supposedly they're retired from Random House and loaded."

"I was at Surely You Jest yesterday."

"I wasn't—too scared." She pulled a tissue from her bodice and blew.

"Charlie spent five minutes calling my efforts crappy and too sentimental, dubbed me a creator of cesspools too murky to edit, then switched to saying the manuscript for my next book contains must-read treasures. Who knows what he thinks?"

"Why do we put up with him?" Vanessa jerked the brim of her hat.

"Ego, isn't it? Who's going to read our work in ten years? No one. I was supposed to hurry home, edit my new collection for the seventh time, format it according to Pooh-bah's *Author's Guide*, and attach the file to an e-mail. Instead, I sat brooding on a bench in the Plaza by the bandstand, then walked down here for a bowl of gazpacho and croissant."

Vanessa reached to lay a warm palm on his forearm. "We could self-publish. Why not? Xlibris and iUniverse and Amazon's CreateSpace make it easy, my best friend tells me. She's done a book with each already."

"So why is she talking to the couple up on Tano?"

"Ego, ego, ego, ego, you're right. There's still more cachet to having someone else publish you. It smoke screens the truth that we publish to be noticed: look at me, I'm important, what I write can change your *life*. But it's all so exhausting, this coming up with yet another reason to leave bed for yet another day."

"Doesn't the writing itself, though, make us somehow feel grounded?"

"It does. It does that." She set her eyes full on his face. "What's your name?"

"Seymour Sabatini."

"May I look at your book?"

"May I buy you an early dinner?"

"What? Oh, I don't know. When?

"Tonight? We can talk more freely. Say five-thirty, Il Vicino?"

"I have no plans."

"Good!" Seymour opened *Mayor Daley, Bye-Bye* to the title page. "You're Vanessa?"

"Vanessa Z. Nord."

Seymour unclipped a ballpoint, scribbled the date and *To Vanessa with pleasure from Seymour Sabatini*, and presented her with the signed copy propped in both hands. He stood. "I'd love to buy anything you've published. Bring something, will you? I'd better go pay Troll-Trevor and start trudging through the formatting chores Charlie's asked me to get started on."

6

Getting Real

In the news:

Hotter temperatures, fitful gusts slow firefighters' efforts to contain New Mexico's largest wildfire ever, charring more than 233 square miles since June 26. "That one area where we had 40,000 acres go in a day included dozens of homes," said a spokeswoman for the Santa Fe National Forest.

In Afghanistan, 1,462 civilians died between January and June this year, UN officials claim. Taliban suicide attacks and roadside bombings caused half of the fatalities. Airstrikes from US Apache helicopters accounted for 79 additional civilian deaths.

Standard & Poors predicts a 50 per chance of downgrading the US government's credit rating within three months, marking the agency's second warning in the past two days.

New Mexico's governor Susana Martinez announces $10,000 reward to the first participant in a web-based contest to present William Bonney, alias Billy the Kid, with an arrest warrant. People can download clues as to his whereabouts from the Catch-the-Kid smartphone application.

Charlie swung his zero-to-sixty-in-five-point-two seconds, twin-turboed black Mercedes from Montezuma Avenue into the lot facing Pranzo Italian Grill.

"Which space do you think, Possum?"

"Watch it!" Benji righted himself. His body twitched with the leather seat's automated massage. "What's the rush?"

"Foolio poontang, gotta claim our booth before the Tashes show up."

"How come?" Benji asked.

"Gives us the power, dum-dum."

Benji resettled granny glasses that the massage had jiggled aslant. "There's a slot, between the red whatchamacallit and that battered-up Chevy."

"No thanks." Charlie slowed, squinted into sunlight turning the elms' dried leaves bronze. "There. At the end. Just beyond the van."

"Don't see it yet."

"Fiddlesticks and bandercock, what do you wear those goggles for? There! There! Beside that bush with the orange berries."

"Don't yell at me, bud."

Behind them the driver of a Range Rover honked.

"I'm trying to find a safe harbor, shithole." Surely You Jest's publisher inched forward over pools of light gleaming from the hot asphalt.

Another blast came from the Rover.

Charlie flipped the driver the finger, then wheeled in beside the van. The Rover rushed past.

"That bush has thorns on it, Charlie."

"Am I too close?" He paddle-shifted into Park.

"Let's see." Benji pulled the door handle.

"Don't step on the sill! I have to polish all four of those buggers every week."

"You're fine."

"Let's hop, then." Charlie removed the key and climbed out.

In the minute it took to reach the restaurant, the ambient eighty-eight degrees had dampened Charlie's boxers and under the arms of the sport shirt printed with bamboo that he, like Benji, wore. He held the glass door marked *Happy Hour Seven Days* and followed his assistant into the cool, wishing the kid's ponytail didn't swish so.

From the bar came the scent of Chianti.

"You saved our booth?" Charlie asked the overly plump hostess.

She consulted the notebook on the rostrum. "Charles Small? Party of four?"

"Yes and yes."

"Oh, wow, those red suspenders. What do they say?" She bent close, dreamcatcher earrings swinging.

"*Santa Fe 400 Years*. My associate's got them, too."

"Cool. Your table, gents. Welcome to Pranzo."

Charlie scooted close to the wall, where one of a dozen brass nameplates read *Surely You Jest Press*. "Sit opposite, Possum. I want the wife next to me. Joe goes by you." He unwrapped the napkin from the silverware, patted the back of his neck, draped the napkin across his thigh.

Half the booths and tables-set-for-four had filled. Charlie pulled out his father's watch.

"They're late."

"Settle down, boss."

"You brought the stevia?"

"I... forgot." Benji raised his eyebrows as he stared across.

"Pookie jabronie, can't I trust you to do any old thing?"

"Look in the dish. Maybe . . . "

"Ahh." Charlie shoved aside the tray holding olive oils to grab up a handful of packets. He fanned them across the linen—*Splenda, SweetFiber, Ultra, Equal, Indulge, Shape, Turbinado Sugar, Sweet 'N Low*—pink, yellow, green, pale blue, white.

"Something to start, gentlemen?" The young man in a hairnet, birthmark browning a bit of skin above his eye, gathered the sweeteners into a pile to allow room for two menus and a basket of bread.

"You've got stevia?" Charlie twisted the Old Miss class ring around his pinkie.

"Stevia, sir?"

"An herb of the sunflower family. Leaves are three hundred times sweeter than sugar but good for you, the best, comes in packets like these, only purple-and-white. Nope, you don't. Can see by your expression." He handed up the wine list. "We won't need this. Two iced coffees, yes?"

Benji nodded.

"And a couple of two-percent milks. And here comes Joe's mate." Charlie patted the cushion beside him.

Jane Tash showed up in Bermudas and a pullover blouse with lacy, elbow-length sleeves. A New Mexican primrose perched above the auburn twist that hung over a breast. As she lowered herself, the flower fell onto the sweeteners. Charlie snatched it up and poked the stem back into her hair.

"Hello," said the waiter, returning with iced coffees, two-percent, and a third menu.

"Have you ordered?" Jane asked Benji.

"Waiting for you." Charlie placed his palm on her wrist. "Where's your husband?"

After asking for water, she freed her hand to open the menu. "When we got home yesterday, he napped, then—though he knows better—turned on his Bloombergs before dinner. Bank of America, Hewlett-Packard, and the manufacturer of Blackberry, I forget the name, had tanked. He'd invested us heavily. And I'd fixed chile rellenos especially. This morning he wouldn't leave bed. 'Oh, foo! How are we going to promote the book?' I asked him. 'Copper and soybeans,' he said."

"Huh?"

"I believe we told you. He headed up commodity trades at Goldman Sachs before we left the east coast. Joe knows his stuff. Used to, anyway."

"Let's pretend," Benji said.

"Zip it, Possum. Of course he knows his stuff."

The waiter, who'd reappeared, set down Jane's water, started to gather up the sweeteners.

"Not so fast, buster. A few minutes?" Charlie asked.

Black apron fluttering, the waiter strode to a table in the big room's center where one of three men sat signaling him.

"Benji, what'll we have? Gluten-free, no lactose."

"I know that."

"Memory plays tricks. Caesar with salmon?"

"Looks pretty good."

"Or splurge in honor of our author—" Charlie turned to cup Jane's elbow—"with the filet mignon on mixed greens?"

"Could do that."

"No, I think the salmon. Add soup? We've got a long afternoon ahead. Wonder what the soup is?"

"Shall we ask?"

"Not sure. Filet and greens, want to?"

"Fine, Charlie."

"No cause to snap. I'll get a few more of these SweetFibers. Seem safe enough." He threw the rest of the pastel packets into their dish. "Gabbling too long. We're here to celebrate you and Joe. Our collaboration is going to make us all rich or I miss my guess. Desolate that Joe's under the weather but we want you to chow down. Anything."

Jane frowned across at him, bit a nail, looked back at the menu. "I think the insalada caprese. And black coffee."

"Black. Really. Yep, creating a book as important as yours is no picnic. We know all about that, don't we, Benji?"

The younger man nodded, deciding silence could best cage the unexpected jealousy swelling inside him.

"Enough time?" asked the waiter, fishing a pad from his apron.

Charlie conveyed their orders. "And a couple more SweetFibers."

"Jane," he asked when the waiter had left, "did you bring a calendar?"

"You told us to at the meeting yesterday and I did." She extracted it from her shoulder bag.

"Good-o. iPad, Possum?"

Benji unsnapped the holster on his belt.

"We need to agree on a date for the cover shoot. What about two weeks from now, last Sunday in July?"

"My son and I attend church."

"Of course. As you should. Afterwards?" How he wished she hadn't rimmed her eyes like a raccoon nor used so much lip gloss.

"That might work."

"Say two o'clock, using the meadow you talked about fronting your place? Make us a map. Benji will contact some of our authors, tell 'em to round up the wagons. Right, Benji?"

"Right." The younger man's eyes darted to Jane's.

"We couldn't hear you," Charlie said.

"Right!"

Charlie turned to Jane, threw his thumb up. "Benji'll be doing the shooting, hi-de-ho. The rest of the live bodies'll be surrounding his joke car because its yellow's so cheery—hopeful, like you said—and its black's so somber, like our future if we don't get a move on. You'll be holding up a sign of condensed chapter headings, Candy's job to make. *You Can Save Us All* in Clarendon caps with *Reverence for Life* and *Detach With Love* below, followed by your and Joe's names. On the diagonal, *Time to Act* or *High Time to Act* or *The Time to Act is Now.*"

"I have to agree with our neighbor, Marta Means. It sounds awfully cluttered," Jane said.

"Not to worry. Candy can work miracles with InDesign."

"Everyone dresses as if for church?" she asked.

"Yesterday your hubby said yes and so did we—tell us more about his troubles, will you? How did they start? We need him healthy."

Jane found herself weeping as she recounted her, Joe's, and Herk's lives following Tatum's death. She declined the hankie Charlie offered, dabbed her eyes with her own.

The ambient chatter had doubled when the waiter finally strode back into view, bearing two caesars with salmon and one insalada caprese on a round tray. He distributed the plates. "Anything else I can get you?"

"What's this?" Charlie asked.

The waiter considered his order pad. "Your caesar with salmon, sir."

"Did I not say put the dressing on the side?"

"Looks like I didn't write that down."

"And did I not say balsamic, not Caesar?"

"I guess I didn't hear you."

"I can't tolerate lactose."

"I'll make the exchange, sir."

"Balsamic on the side except the lady's. And hurry up, I'm famished. So is my partner."

Partner now, Benji wondered?

The hairnetted waiter placed the two caesar salads on his tray and left.

"What in a rat's cloaca is this place up to hiring help that has no inkling of the finesse needed to serve the public, expecting us regulars to bow while incompetence beats us over the heads?" Charlie began to wheeze, folded his hands on the tablecloth, and bent to gaze at them.

"You'll have to excuse the boss," Benji told Jane.

Face flushing, he jerked his head up. "Eat, eat!"

"We've been under a lot of pressure," Benji said. "This morning Seymour Sabatini called—you met him Monday, the guy with the double mustache?"

"I remember." Jane forked up a bite of mozzarella and tomato.

"We've lost a major tenant and Seymour, who made quite a bundle in real estate in Chicago, has promised to find us a replacement. Knows people here in high places. But this morning he told Charlie that, in exchange for the favor, he expects us to advance the pub date of his second book of poems. And before that, to hustle another book out."

"By her highness," Charlie muttered. "Vanessa Z. Nord. A Jewish princess if there ever was one."

"Don't think she's Jewish," Benji said.

"No princess, either," Charlie said. "A she-wolf and blackmailer." He ripped open the lone packet of SweetFiber, and shook it into his coffee. "Means I'll have to publish them both before you. They've already submitted their cover art—boring. Paintings. But no prob. We'll get your book out lickety-split anyhow." He slipped one hand under the tablecloth and, wrinkling it upward, found Jane's knee.

She pushed his hand aside. "May we keep everything on a professional level? I'd appreciate it."

"What are you talking about?" Charlie asked while Benji sat watching them, fuming.

"You know exactly what I'm—ah."

The waiter appeared around the corner carrying two salads.

"Here you are, gentlemen. I'm embarrassed by the mix-up. Buon gusto."

"Looks okay," Charlie said. He poured oil on the slice of focaccia from the basket.

Wishing she were home, Jane asked for more black coffee.

"We forgot yesterday to talk back-cover blurbs," Charlie said, sprinkling balsamic onto his romaine.

"I've e-mailed Lester Brown."

"Who?"

"The man who wrote *Mobilizing to Save Civilization*. We quote him in our intro."

"You've heard of him, Benji?"

A bite of salmon halfway to his mouth, Benji shrugged.

"And thought I'd ask our neighbor, Marta Means," Jane said.

"She's well known in Santa Fe, anyway," Charlie said.

Instead of Marta, Jane found herself yearning to ask Rolf Goodenough, her Tea Party compatriot, for the second blurb. "Life's absurd," she said.

"Oh, indeed. And on that subject, as we abandon the printed page for now-you-see-it, now-you-don't virtual reality, allow me to list what you get by paying a mere hundred bucks for e-book access." Charlie sliced off a sliver of salmon, stabbed a bit of romaine, lifted them into his mouth, chewed, swallowed. "Nook, iPad, iPhone—help me, Benji—Kindle, Kobo, Sony Reader—all can take your manuscript because we format it on ePub, don't ask me how. Ask Benji—not now. The possum's in a funk over golly jeepers who knows what? Missing his cat?"

"What I miss is courtesy." Benji gulped down most of his iced coffee as the septuagenarian watched his assistant's Adam's apple bob.

The waiter brought Jane's refill, and two more SweetFibers—too late. Charlie, Benji, and she finished their luncheon pretty much in silence.

After Charlie had paid and Jane rose, he slid across the cushion and embraced her.

"Like to give our new authors a good-luck hug. Never mind. The next step is to bring me quick as a wink a perfectly formatted CD of your manuscript. No flash drives, they're too often fouled up with manufacturers' promotions."

"I'll ask Joe to help. I've got to—"

"You're in a hurry to leave us?"

"Lots to do."

What she needed most to do was pee. She passed the receptionist's rostrum and vanished into the hall.

Benji followed Charlie across the restaurant's burnt-brick apron to the street's other side. As they passed under an elm, he reached to yank toward him the back crossover of Charlie's suspenders, then let go. The elastic snapped against shirt's bamboo.

Wincing, Charlie wheeled as Benji stepped backwards off the curb.

"What in hellikers was that for?"

"Because you're an asshole, Charlie."

"For my comment about your cat? I can't help what I say sometimes, you've learned that."

"Short Stuff's content with my office door closed. She's got her water and kibbles and poop box."

"What then?" Charlie swung his hand to press the stinging flesh that covered his kidney. He felt the shirt dampening.

"Coming on to Jane Tash."

"I get caught up in adrenaline—I'm sweating here, Benji boy. Let's move it, huh? Huh?"

"I need a committed relationship, Charlie, if I'm going to think about coming to live at your place. No fooling around with women. I'm serious about this, mister."

Charlie brushed his still-thick hair, thumbed a suspender strap off his chest, saw Buck Monk's body seven years ago in the Las Campanas hacienda, limp on their queen-size bed. "Got to be a two-way street, Possum. Meaning show me you're ready for a commitment."

"Like just how?"
"Give your landlord of that rattrap garage notice tonight."

7

Charlie's Second Ex

In the news:

A 19-year-old female driver died after failing to yield to oncoming traffic when turning left off NM 599 onto Country Road 62. This was the second fatality this summer at that intersection. In a third accident, a man lost his arm.

Twenty-two people were killed yesterday in suburbs of Damascus, the highest daily toll there since the nationwide uprising began in April. "Where has my brother gone, where are my granddaughters?" asks Maria Khalaf. The violence has now taken nearly 75,000 lives.

The federal government is pondering selling off gold in Fort Knox, plus buildings and acreage from national parklands, should Congress and President Obama fail to agree to increase America's borrowing limit. This marks the third time Congress has proposed selling off real estate to reduce federal debt.

Facebook, the world's largest social network at 750 million users, has begun partnering with Skype to offer live video chats for free. Twitter and LinkedIn are also reported to be on the hunt for phone-substitute partners.

❖ ❖ ❖

"**W**atch it, kiddie pomp!"

Charlie thumbed his horn at the woman in short-shorts and a green ribbon that fluttered in the hot, Sunday-evening breeze. She jerked the curtained stroller back and he wheeled onto Calle Anna Jean south of the state library, braking the Mercedes in front of the home of Kittie Rehmeyer, his former second wife.

Charlie rented her the two-bedroom adobe, on the corner of Carlos Rey, for $1,100 a month. Recently, he'd paid to top the chainlink-and-slat fence with barbed wire because twice since Christmas someone had forced the gate to snip a foot-square hole in her American flag. It flapped from a pole near polypropylene pink flamingos that a client who lived in Tampa had given her when she and he became lovers long ago, following the breakup with Charlie.

Hot air was dampening Charlie's armpits and the backs of his knees—he'd had to leave all of the coupe's windows cracked to rope a drainpipe to the quilt covering the sunroof.

He loosened his safety belt and untied the knots hovering over front and rear seats. The red rag he'd attached to the pipe's end waved as he stepped out in fishnet polo and khakis torn at the knees, opened the rear door, and took up tool kit, keyhole saw, electric drill, and caulking gun.

He managed to keep them from falling while walking under the bird feeders toward the front door, cursing himself for yielding to Kittie's plea, even though she had been Surely You Jest's CPA ever since he bought the press. He squinted at the setting sun shooting rays through the Siberian elms, kindling the rental's gutters.

A UPS truck rattled past the corner as the home's front door opened.

"Hello, Choo-choo."

Kittie stood under the awning, hands on capri-clad hips. Her green-framed glasses matched a dirt-splotched shirt, its sleeves rolled to the elbows. Unlike Charlie, she did not color her hair—gray and worn in a bob. She smelled of wet soil. "Have you left enough time before dark?"

"Depends how bad the leak is."

"I'll show you. Excuse the outfit. Been deepening the basins around the butterfly bushes."

"Once I thought you and I would be living here forever."

"Then you met Buck at the classic car powwow."

"I wanted you both," Charlie said, for-the-present convinced.

"Buck died and you set your eye on Benji. Out of the way, please."

Overhead, a propeller noisily drew a small plane west. Kittie pushed past and walked along the drive to where a honey locust overhung the garage. She pointed up at the canale.

Charlie carried his tools toward her. "You would have taken me back?"

"Water over the dam. I see you found a drainpipe."

"Wrigglety-piggety, I should have had you pay someone to do this. Took me hours going through Big Jo's and Lowes until I found the pipe at Home Depot—hey, they rhyme!"

A flatbed hauling 2x6s rumbled along Carlos Rey. Charlie dropped kit and tools on the cracked cement, headed for the Mercedes, and lifted the ribbed pipe off the quilt, which he folded and set on the back seat. He jumped in front, careful not to let his work boots touch the sill, revved the engine, raised the windows, turned the key, left the car and locked it, lifted the pipe and brought it to where Kittie waited. "When did you find your mailbox bashed?"

"Last Tuesday. And I left work early to undergo a background check for a .38 pistol which I keep in the silverware drawer. I'll bring the ladder."

"And an extension cord."

"You always were better at fix-up than any of the handymen we hired. I bet secretly you still enjoy doing it."

Charlie watched her butt recede toward the garage's side door. Still a good-looking tomato. If Benji keeps stalling against moving to my place, he thought, maybe I should see if Kittie would like to. I'd let her break her lease. Las Companas is a lot safer.

When she returned and stood the ladder against the wall, Charlie took her elbow. "Will you help me out with a cover shoot?"

"You want to change the cover of my book?"

"Foolio poontang, Kittie, no way." He pulled his earlobe. "Black-and-white of you youngish, hopscotching? Perfect. And a more-than-perfect title."

"Let me go, Choo-choo."

He obeyed as though her elbow had turned white hot.

"I have you to thank," Kittie said. "Who else could have come up with *You Did Good, Girl: How to Hopscotch into a Hopeful Relationship after You're Sixty*?"

"You're too adept a writer to keep spending eight to five all these years slaving over clients' monthly accounts. Though for sure I'm grateful you do."

"Why are you flattering me?"

"Rather I made fun?" Charlie asked. "Like Benji and I did Thursday? Thinking you could correct in red a PDF file and e-mail it back? Dum-dum

Kittie, you have to print out the file, correct that, and *snail mail* the corrected pages."

"I did!"

"After Benji phoned you."

Kittie clenched her eyes not to take a swing at him. "The sun's leaving us, buddy boy."

"And I'm going up." He disengaged the extension's hooks, slid the aluminum skyward until its end passed the leaking canale, and began his climb. "Oh: tools."

"I'll bring them."

"Once the book's published," he shouted, "you'll be getting offers enough to make those beautiful eyes spin."

She picked up the steel box, saw, drill, and caulking gun.

"Or do you already have someone in your life I don't know about?"

"Flamingos and flickers all year long, black-chinned hummers and towhees in the spring."

He mopped his forehead with the back of a hand and dropped his arm. "Gimme the drill and plug the cord in."

She complied.

"You should dye your hair before *You Did Good* comes out," Charlie said.

"You dare tell me what to do? Somebody wants a girlfriend, he takes this one as she is, lonely and growing old."

Before reaching the step where he could comfortably bore holes, Charlie said, "You may be aging, but me? Immortal. All is Infinite Mind, I'm just its manifestation."

"You're just the prize at the bottom of a box of Crackerjack. I thought you gave up Christian Science after Buck died."

"Swing back and forth, depending on my mood."

Sorrowing for a moment that Kittie and he had split up thirteen years ago, he triggered the drill and bored four holes through the canale's underside to mark the corners of a rectangle. He'd forgotten to bring goggles. Though he tilted his head away, sawdust rained into his eyes and between the black threads of his shirt's fishnet.

"Go fetch water!"

"Fetch?" Kittie guffawed.

"My eyes are on fire."

She hurried through the front door and seconds later emerged holding the handle of a small plastic bucket. She climbed up and exchanged it for the drill. One hand clutched a rung, the other grasped the bucket's rim and jerked. Water splashed his face, dousing his eyes. She tossed the rest at him, released the bucket to bounce off the concrete.

"Saw!"

She'd thought to bring a dish towel, handed it over, descended as he dried off. In the dusk she climbed three rungs again to hand him the saw.

Using the towel to shield against sawdust, he commenced to cut from hole to hole. The rectangle of rotting wood fell. He dropped the saw after it. "That cover shoot I mentioned? Two Sundays after tomorrow. Two o'clock. For a hot new manuscript, *You Can Save Us All.*"

"Save us from what?"

Ourselves, he thought, as a dry-cleaner's van rattled out of sight. He turned to watch the sun dapple in purple and salmon the spaces among leaves quaking above the tar-and-gravel roofs—and found himself wishing he were seven again, walking home swinging a string bag bulging with groceries, knowing his mother would reward him with kisses for fetching them, would call him "my best errand boy."

"What's the manuscript about, Choo-choo?"

He twisted to look down. "Make-believe stuff. Slow global warming, change our mind-sets, treat each other kindly, think of our grandchildren, that sort of thing. But fiddlesticks and bandersnatch, you never know, do you? May have some effect, can't hurt. And the authors say they've saved megabucks to promote it. Surely You Jest can surely use the dough. I spoke out of turn a couple of weeks back, pissed off Sotheby's top dog. He's taking his crew and decamping."

"That's not good news, Choo-choo. This recession/depression isn't going away soon. Your last month's balance sheet looked pretty shaky. You've always had a big mouth."

"You know when I feel cornered I can't help what comes out."

"Pooh. You're just spoiled. Why not, I'll be in your cover shoot."

"You gotta dress as though heading for church. Authors' demand."

"I dress like that Monday through Friday."

"Sexpot in sheep's clothing? No less than when we married. Hand me the drainpipe, let's see if the end fits. It's getting dark—maybe wait until tomorrow to come caulk and secure it."

"There's a thunderstorm predicted tonight."

"Then hustle that pipe up." Gusts had begun cooling his chest and neck.

The pipe squealed skyward along the rungs until its curved bottom rested in her hands. Charlie grabbed the other end, began worrying it into the opening he'd created.

"Goddamn, Choo-choo!"

"What?" He startled at the governor's helicopter overhead, click-click-ing its way north.

"You should have warned me."

"About what?" He peered down. She held the pipe's end in one hand, clamped an elbow to her ribs for support, and shook her other hand. Blood whirled out.

"Hold the hand high, Kit!"

"The raw end dug into me." She lowered it to lay on the drive, then raised the wounded hand to a Statue-of-Liberty pose. It flopped from her wrist. The blood trickled down.

When he reached her, he pulled her arm to where he could wrap the hand in the dishtowel. "We'll drench it in hydrogen peroxide."

"Throbbing pretty bad, Choo-choo."

Before propelling her toward the front door, he flung his arm around her shoulder and kissed her cheek.

She stiffened. "What was that for?"

"I want us to try again. I still have feelings for you."

"Ménage à trois with your assistant?"

"Might work, Kittie."

"You bastard! Get away!"

Clouds had overcast the darkening sky and the wind had steadied. Raindrops spattered their arms.

"Forgot my tools!" Charlie hurried back to the ladder's foot to unplug the drill, grab up it, the steel box, caulking gun, and saw. "I'll meet you inside."

"No way in hell." As he passed her toward the Mercedes, she drew her right arm back and smacked his head, catching the base of his skull. The loose tools clattered to the concrete.

"You're suggesting a triangle for us? You're no bi, you're a gay man, you spent eleven years in the sack with Dr. Buck Monk. Leave us women alone. In this town that embraces gayness, pretending you're not? Pathetic. Be honest for once."

She swiped raindrops from her bob. "How do you think Benji would feel if he knew you were coming onto your CPA?"

"He doesn't even know you and I were married."

"What's his not knowing have to do with anything?"

Charlie set the toolbox on the dampened drive, piled drill, saw, and gun on top, and hoisted the bunch. "I'll be over tomorrow."

"And you're a dead man if you dare to."

8

Cover Shoot

In the news:

Spaceport America, 75 miles southwest of the Trinity atomic-bomb site and a year behind schedule, will cater mostly to the rich. Already 400 folks have pledged $200,000 each to rocket 50,000 feet into suborbital space on billionaire Richard Branson's SpaceShip Two.

Game officials recently okayed trapping or snaring the Mexican gray wolf, on the endangered species list since 1976. Regional Fish and Wildlife's Tom Buckley suggests checking traps regularly so that the wolves and other creatures needn't suffer overmuch.

Lupita and Lourdes are among seven siblings living here as undocumented immigrants. They walked eight hours through the Sonoran Desert, then paid $2,000 each to cram with four others into a panel truck for the hot, 600-mile ride northeast to Santa Fe.

Dear Daphne: Collections can quickly become overwhelming, yet it's a shame not to display them. Grouping your model cars and funky necklaces together is a fine example of eclecticism. Tip: use a level or plumb bob to precisely position every treasure. *Hints from Heloise*

On the last Sunday in July, Charlie, Joe, Jane, and Herk stood at quarter of two beside Charlie's Mercedes in the meadow that fronted the Tashes' Tesuque home. The Bermuda and buffalo grass smelled like mown hay in the hot sun. On the branch of a cottonwood, a black-headed grosbeak whistled its sixteenth-note riff.

Jane and Herk had kept on the outfits they'd worn to Holy Faith that morning, Jane in a paisley, scoop-neck dress that nicely showed off a Kokopelli fashioned from jasper, fluting below her collarbones. Shadow and liner darkened her eyes, a bright pink sparked her lips.

In contrast to the plum-colored shirt Herk pressed last night, hoping Candy would be part of today's gathering, Joe had insisted on the black rayon pullover he always struggled into when his twin Bloombergs showed commodities falling.

"Well, hickory moly belladonna, she appears!" Charlie exclaimed. Not planning to show up in the photo, he wore the fishnet polo and khakis torn at the knees he'd donned to install the drainpipe at Kittie Reymeyer's rental two weeks ago.

"Who appears?" Jane asked.

"Our CPA. I haven't heard from her for a fortnight."

"What's weird about that, except use of the word?" Herk looked along the stone wall to the old Saab convertible, red enamel firing off glints of sunshine. It turned past the swung-back gate.

"You make too many queries," Charlie told Herk.

"I only asked—"

"Too many." Charlie picked his way toward Kittie, standing among the pasteboard signs displaying chapter heads that Candy had colored and staple-gunned to stakes. He'd spread them face up on the grass to imply to the cover-shoot's participants how important giving their best this afternoon was to *You Can Save Us All*'s success. He paused to whisk a katydid off his hair. The insect whirred toward the Mercedes and dropped between a couple of New Mexican primroses.

Kittie emerged in a frilled, white blouse and nearly-see-through skirt printed with poinsettias. She'd tied a green scarf the shade of her glasses' frames around her neck. Charlie stepped forward, making a vee of his arms to hug her, but she pushed him away.

"I'm here because I want you to publish me, okay? And I need you to help me format the damn thing. I don't think the way your *Guide for Authors* wants me to. Plus I'd like to hold onto your bookkeeping business. Where's our cameraman?"

"On his way from an Overeaters Anonymous get-together."

"Yike! This grass is full of little stinging thingies." Kittie bent to scratch a well-turned ankle above her two-inch-heeled leather pump.

"You haven't called me Choo-choo yet," Charlie whispered.

"And I'm not going to."

"This is our CPA," he told the others, preceding Kittie. "Benji should be along soon."

"And wearing black fishnet and khakis torn at the knees, anyone care to bet?" Herk asked.

Nearly as tall as her son, Jane grabbed his elbow and shook it.

"Herk," Joe suggested, "why don't you go sketch the creek?"

"Because Candy may come."

"Riddly ruminators, Hulk, our art director's at her piano lesson. It's Sunday."

"I'll go sketch the creek."

Jane hooked his belt. "Baby, don't do that. I want you on our cover."

A white Corvette convertible appeared on the long drive to the gate. It spun gravel accelerating through. Beyond the split-rail fence Marta's three mares began to pace, snorting. The largest, piebald, pried his way past the others and galloped toward the gabled, aluminum roof of a home a football field away. Marta had just stepped onto her porch.

Vanessa waited in the Corvette until Seymour had hopped out, rounded the rear end, and opened the door for her. The multimillionaire sonneteer had arrayed himself in a Stetson circled by conchos holding a partridge feather, a cream-colored untucked guayabera, jeans, and alligator boots. Vanessa rose in peach organdy imprinted with chickadees. She spotted grape hyacinths growing near a bench, rushed over to pluck one, poked it into her mass of auburn hair.

"You two are together?" asked Charlie, crinkling his eyes and wiping his forehead.

The split between Seymour's twin mustaches widened as he grinned and nodded. Vanessa took his arm.

"Listen: you want your manuscripts published fast? Then don't, I repeat don't, as you did Friday, hand me CDs that are formatted *wrong*. That's crap, people. First item in the *Guide for Authors* says, *Make sure the show/hide function button is turned* on *so you can see paragraph and space marks.* Most important first step—and you *forgot*. Come by tomorrow, we'll go over the guide together, though I am not your nursemaid, I'm publisher." He grasped front and back bills of the Sherlock Holmes cap Benji had bought him for their first-ever photo shoot together two years ago.

"Mighty Pooh-Bah's finished?"

Vanessa shrank half a step behind Seymour. The top-heavy hyacinth fell past the mole above her eye to her shoulder, then to an espadrille.

"Follow author guidelines!" Charlie's voice softened as fast as it had risen. "Goes for cover art CDs, too. We're here now—and thanks for helping out, you know I mean that—to come up with a photo for a life-preserving treatise."

"Pales in importance to hers and mine, chum," Seymour retorted. "Poetry changes everything."

"Humbugger! Too much poesy already. And your own cover art CDs are *not* acceptable resolution. We need TIF files, three-hundred resolution. JPEGS are too low for full color. TIFs, not JPEGs, and the guidelines say no e-mails." Charlie's voice rose. "No e-mails, no voice mails! You reach us *live*—not me. Funnel everything through Benji."

"Quit the yelling, huh? It upsets the ladies. To get Vanessa's and my next collection published, I'm going to save your financial ass—talking with a maybe-lessee right now." Seymour squeezed Vanessa's fingers. "My girl and I'll find you what you need. Tit for tat—no offense, sweetie." He twitched his mustache against her cheek.

Jane, Joe, and Herk had retreated to the bench under a clutch of aspen. "Oh!" Jane cried out, "Oh, good, Marta has decided to join us."

"SYJ's official peacemaker," Charlie managed between wheezes. He removed his hat and patted his hair with a handkerchief drawn from his back pocket. "Fiddlefart, I hate it when the Possum's late—okeydokey, here he is, with Mad Dog in hot pursuit."

Benji's bumblebee-striped MINI Cooper sprayed dust over Rolf's two-year-old Hummer. Someone had added paintings to the behemoth's olive green. The vehicles bounced into the meadow under darkening clouds.

Marta fed a carrot to each horse and headed for the stile she'd had Herk build for her. She mounted it in chocolate skirt cut to mid-thigh and lavender blouse, grasped her soft-brimmed hat and the safety pole Herk had screwed to the stile's top, reversed her direction, and clambered down.

Joe told Jane sotto voce, "I need to talk to you."

"What about? Hi, dear! Thanks so much—"

"Of course," Marta said, then turned to Charlie. "Hello, Charles. Can we finish up by four? Jane and I've got an interview with a couple, possible new housekeeper and gardener for us to share. I've been advertising the apartment over my garage."

Charlie stared at her, rotating the Old Miss ring around his pinky as a Cooper's hawk flapped out of a Siberian elm.

Joe pushed his lips to his wife's ear. "Jane?"

She backed away and faced him. "What? What?"

"My bunion's killing me and the gut's started to spasm. It's the heat."

"Go park on the bench, take your shoes off, and calm down. Did you bring your jerky along?"

Wincing, he nodded.

"Well?"

He hauled out the already-opened packet, bit off a plug, and hobbled to the aspen.

Benji stopped in an open patch of grass and stepped from his MINI.

"Told you," Herk said.

"Told us what?" Jane asked.

"The helper: Black fishnet polo and khakis, minus the detective cap. And hey, only one knee ripped. These two guys are lovers."

Hearing Herk's remark, Benji paused, Nikon D70S looped around his neck.

Kittie raised her brows, guffawed, and skipped sideways to a patch of dirt. "Less buggie things here maybe."

No one else spoke.

Dressed for the occasion in a cufflinked, red-, white-, and blue-checked shirt, Mad Dog passed by his front bumper. Its plate read *The Truth Since 32 A.D.*, followed by a Christian cross. "Howdy, all," he growled. "Chas, assume that lynch-scene cover CD I mailed in met your expectations?"

Charlie stayed silent, turned his gaze again to Herk.

"Hey. Nothing wrong with gayness. I've toyed with the idea myself. Santa Fe's a hotbed. Many of my friends in New York..."

Rolf wheeled. "Adios, all, if pederasty's the subject."

But Jane moved between him and her son. "Herk, baby, doing a little sketching's maybe a good idea?"

"Best yet," Joe called from the bench.

"And don't come back till the crickets start chirping," Charlie said.

"I'll deal with this if you don't mind," Jane said.

"Fiddle-dee-dee, I do. But no way I'm going to honor the pork's slur with a retort." Charlie called over his shoulder, "Benji, bring the camera?"

He faced Jane's son again. "Trot off so we can proceed."

"Herk?" Jane asked. "You don't have to—"

"Yeah? Seems like first you want me here, then you don't. This project is all such pie in the sky anyway." He strode toward his casita.

Before Jane could decide whether or not to chase after him, Rolf approached. "Hello, ma'am. Too much commotion for hot weather, agreed?" He doffed his Stetson. "Mighty glad to see you."

Now Marta hurried to Jane through the grass, crushing a clump of primroses. "Which sign shall I carry?"

"Marta, just a minute, I need to ask this gentleman a question." She bit a fingernail. "It's personal, Marta."

"Oh? I'll go ask Charles how I can help set up." The tip of her long nose twitched.

Jane felt her crotch warm and wondered why this scarecrow's scent of tobacco stimulated her so. Plus the way Rolf grasped the brim of his hat to tilt it further to the left. "Would you be willing to write a blurb for my husband's and my book? I've asked someone on the east coast, too, and if he won't or you won't, guess I'll ask Marta."

"Myself be mighty honored, ma'am." Mad Dog dipped his chin.

"Don't know you'll agree with everything in the text."

"Let's bet those gorgeous eyes I will. You and I're friends of Mark and Jenny Beth, yes?"

"Yes, oh, yes! I'll run into the house and get you a copy of the manuscript and put it in that rather amazing vehicle you drove here. Those scenes on your car, can they be stations of the cross?"

"Can be and are. My boy enameled them, sides, back, top, hood. Two coats. He graduates next May with a minor in fine art from Chattanooga Baptist. Tell you what. Give me a few days with your treatise and come on by. I've been itching to start up a group of the Patriots. Santa Fe has no Tea Party cell yet. Bring your ball-and-chain and your boy."

"My husband's an atheist, I'm afraid, and Herk I doubt—"

"Come along on your own, then. How does Thursday evening sit? I'll rustle us up something tasty and we can brainstorm."

"I'd love to!" He gave the hand she offered an extra squeeze.

She dashed past the aspen and Herk's casita and took the hacienda's slate steps two at a time.

"I'm so sorry, darling," she told Marta after setting the copied manuscript on the Hummer's front seat.

Marta stiffened as Jane embraced her shoulder.

"I know you're angry because I changed my mind. I mean about showing children on the cover. Know you had to disappoint a lot of your mommy-friends. I just couldn't—look, I'm weeping, Marta. So *mortifying*. Tatum's gone, Joe's right. And I'm perspiring all over that beautiful lavender blouse of yours." She bent to retrieve the hat her forearm had flicked off her neighbor's black curls, bent again to lift the staked sign reading *Change Destructive Mind-Sets* from the grass. "You hold this one, will you?"

"Well, golly gee, willy whompers, the lady's ready? Those clouds'll be dumping their goodies any minute." Charlie jumped from where he had been fanning himself on the leather backseat of his Mercedes. Benji eased himself from behind its steering wheel and, camera swinging, stood. So did Joe—gingerly—from under the four aspen.

"You carry *Groups Build Leverage*," Jane told her husband. She hefted the sign from near Seymour's Corvette.

"I'm the one to be handling those." Charlie grabbed the sign from her, shoved it stake-first toward Joe. "Kittie? *Tend Our Gardens*. Vanessa? *Put the Lie to Pascal*—no, *Dressing to Give Pleasure*. No, that's Marta's. Here: *No Time to Dither*. Rolf, you take *Prayer Circles*. Seymour, right up your alley, *Create Win-Win Work*."

"I'm standing next to Vanessa."

"Whatever—wait a minute. Benji and I do the grouping. All of you surround his bumblebee."

"What bumblebee?"

"That jokester car over there. Move it, people. Hop, hop."

"So long as I stand next to Vanessa." Seymour encircled her waist as they led the march to the MINI Cooper.

At the rear, forehead beading, Charlie called, "Jane? You and Joe in front, against the passenger door. The rest form a daisy chain. Skip holding hands, just circle the car."

"That big cloud's causing too much shade, bud," Benji said.

"It'll pass. Fiddlesticks and bandersnatch, this is taking too much time. I want Marta's overbuilt chalet and her cottonwoods in the background. See if you can include the rock wall."

Benji ran from spot to spot, stooped, squinted through the viewfinder. "Can't do it."

Charlie yanked his right earlobe. "Wrigglety-piggety, Possum, forget the wall. Find us a location."

"This works, toward the house, sun at our backs, no glint from the vehicles, maybe catch the heads of those horses if they'll stay put by the fence."

A field mouse leapt from the shade of a back tire. Kittie screamed and hid behind Seymour on the MINI's far side, near its hatchback. Rolf lifted a boot to stomp the rodent. But it raced free toward the bench.

"All right, group, face Benji, make like those signs are grenade launchers, hoist and glower. Vanessa, that's a simper. Wipe it off."

"I need Marta beside me," Jane blurted.

"Thanks for nothing," Joe said.

Jane patted the glass of the window she blocked. "Here, Marta, in front of the side mirror."

Marta left Kittie's side.

"But now I'm just a hood ornament," Kittie said.

"And now we have three front runners!" Charlie fumed. "And Marta has the wrong sign—gimme. *Change Destructive Mind-Sets* was for the pork. Pass it to Jane. Marta, you take *Dressing to Give Pleasure*." An unexpected uprush of grief burnt his throat. Buck, why did you go and die on me? I need you to come home to. "Thrust, people, thrust! The book's serious. *Look* serious. Okay, Benji, open fire."

Charlie's assistant crouched, snapped, Russian-danced to the left, snapped more photos.

"Vanessa, get your hand off your eyes."

"I forgot my sunglasses."

"I don't give a rat's rectum about that."

All of a sudden Kittie started miming a drum majorette, her two-inch heels aerating the buffalo grass-carpeted ground.

"Stop, Possum. What in holy matrimony's the matter with you?"

"Stinging thingies," Kittie said. "I'm in a nest of them."

9

Tea Party Dustup

In the news:

The online bulletin board, *Pleasant Dreams*, was caught sharing videos around the world of sexually abused children under twelve, some of them infants in obvious pain. Seventy-two of the pedophilia club's 600 members have been charged with trading tens of thousands of images.

Inspired by uprisings in Tunisia, pro-democracy rebels in Syria's Hama took to the streets Monday to celebrate the beginning of Ramadan, Islam's holy month. President Bashar Assad has moved tanks into the city, cutting off telephone and Internet service, electricity, food, and some water. In a previous uprising, Assad's father ordered 30,000 killed.

Three days after Santa Fe police locked an electronic anklet on a 12-year-old suspected of stalking an 82-year-old woman, the boy rolled a stolen 2001 Toyota off County Road 56. He appeared yesterday in a jumpsuit, shackled around waist and wrists, to tell Judge Frank Montoya, "I deny the charges."

Nature has just published an explanation of why the dark side of the moon is so hilly. "Fifty billion years ago, we're thinking a smaller moon smashed into it, like a pie in the face," says planetary scientist Eric Asphaug. "We're calling the theory 'the big splat.'"

A cock was crowing so insistently it sounded like several outside Rolf "Mad Dog"'Goodenough's barn when Jane Tash, sucking in air and blowing it out to soothe her nerves, bounced over ruts in her Honda Civic toward Rolf's front gate. Fashioned of wire and rusted tubes, it swung inward from its post.

Light from the six pm sun on this Thursday following Sunday's photo shoot bore through the branches of cottonwoods and elms, causing Jane's eyes to smart even behind dark glasses. She braked, hunched forward, threw her twist of hair over a shoulder, and followed a muddy ditch past an overturned tractor toward the barn. A windmill and water tank loomed to the barn's right rear, near Rolf's home. Should she have come, she wondered, leaving Herk waving and guffawing from the hacienda's top step, Joe closeted inside with his Bloombergs?

The tips of the cock's feathers fluttered red, black, and golden as he herded a clutch of chickens towards a goat roped to a steel stake. Beyond sat Rolf's Hummer, its stations of the cross throwing off sparks as though indeed spiritualized. Nearby grazed a cow.

Before Jane could turn off the engine, a barking German shepherd bounded out the front door. The end of a chain attached to its collar whipped against the porch swing and a couple of Mexican pots before bouncing over the flagstones that led to the Hummer. Jane punched the switch locking her doors and hunkered down below the dash. The bottom of the cross inset with coral and turquoise she'd bought for tonight's rendezvous bit into her chest. Amid barks she could hear the chain whomping the side of her front tire.

"Pussycat, beat it, gimme that!" Rolf yelled. "What's up with you terrifying a guest? Jane, gal, you're safe, the Pussycat's friendly."

She looked up to see Rolf grinning above his cleft chin. A three-cornered blue felt hat in which he'd toothpicked an American flag topped his head. The bare arm he raised in greeting was gaunt and veined, the fingernails long and cracked. He took a hand-rolled cigarette from between chapped lips and stomped it out. He signaled for her to leave the car.

She grabbed her briefcase and a raffia shoulder bag and clambered out.

Rolf lowered Pussycat's chain so that she could sniff the toes poking from Jane's sandals. Jane kicked backward when the dog began to lick.

"But she likes what she sees. Me, too. You're dressed to please a man."

"You said dinner."

"A call for tailored slacks? Pearlized buttons? I needed at least to slip on a bolo tie."

Jane felt her crotch warm. Pussycat circled her as the cock resumed its crowing. She watched the goat lower its head, perhaps to butt the cock, but it hopped out of harm's way.

"They want feeding. I'll be just a moment—oh!"

"Damn." Jane stared at the keys she'd just dropped onto a cow pie.

"Crusted, not to worry." Holding Pussycat's chain, Rolf stooped, rubbed the keys on a patch of grass, handed them to her. "Keep my sidekick, will you?"

Before she could conjure a reason why not, she found herself enduring Pussycat's slobbering while listening to gnats buzz in the heat. Overhead, the clouds were darkening. A Piper Cub droned through an opening toward Santa Fe's airport a mile northeast.

When Rolf returned with a stalk of celery for the goat and a pail of corn, Jane blurted, "I shouldn't be here."

As though to punctuate, thunder boomed while a white half moon continued yellowing above the Sangrias.

"The rightness of your being here's for you to decide. Only woman stuck by me was Shirley, my daughter outside wedlock, cook and house-keeper after I raised her up. Five years ago her bone marrow turned bad. She loved her goat there, Samson. This moment he's straddling her ashes."

Rolf doffed his tricorne at Jane. "For my part, gal, I'm glad you came. What'd your ball-and-chain say?"

"Joe knows I've been faithful."

"So what's the problem, being here?"

"I've never done something like this."

"And I bet never known a literary cowpoke like me. Only planning to eat and gab, aren't we?" He pulled on a corner of his hat. "Found it on eBay—you like? Honoring Mark and Jenny Beth. Those clouds are looking to dump. Let's hustle inside. I'll take Pussycat."

First he lit another cigarette. Bag over her shoulder, briefcase in hand, Jane followed the scent as the trio tramped over the flagstones and up the broad steps. The siding above the screen door Rolf held open displayed a cedar sign, *Real Men Love Jesus.*

She clutched her jeweled crucifix as she entered the living room. It smelled of ribs cooking in the kitchen to the left. Rafters crossed the beam running the length of the sloping ceiling. Rolf released Pussycat and gestured toward the nearest of the sofa's four cushions.

"Beside the Holy Virgin," he said, "ma'am, please."

She sat next to a life-size, plaster rendering of Our Lady of Guadalupe, decked in a blue skirt printed with stars. Plaster rays sprung like gilded spiked hair from a head drooped in prayer. "Your son's work?"

"Freshman project, end of semester. Baptist manufactures the mannequins on campus, Guadalupe, Jesus, Mary, Peter and Paul, Mary Magdalene."

"I'm overwhelmed."

"Properly so."

Strange, he's too strange, Jane thought, at the same time glad she'd rubbed her armpits twice with deodorant. "May I have a look at your books?" she asked.

"If you can get out of that sofa, it's pretty low, far too low for my pegs. Shirley liked to set her Dr. Peppers on those flattened arms."

Pussycat raised herself and followed Jane across the rug to the bookcase, head-high and fashioned from cedar posts that had kept their fragrance, the shelves a lighter-colored wood.

"You have been busy." She gawked at perhaps two dozen titles, face out and wrought in bright-colored script: *Garrison Nails the Shade of Willow Bend, Matt Hayward Guns Down Kit for Keeps, Free-for-All at the Cornstalk Corral, Smile When You Call Me Whore, Miss Daisy Takes Sweet Revenge.* The books' covers, all soft, showed faces in pain or hilarity, surrounded by crags, hills, range grass or meadows. Jane's temples began to hurt.

Pussycat padded to her dish of water under a window that looked out at a vegetable garden. Barbed wire encircled its raised beds. The bitch began to lap, her tongue scattering drops, as Jane returned to the sofa. "You're amazing," she told Rolf, feeling dizzy.

"There's a market for inkslinging like mine." Straight-arming a corner table, Rolf lifted a foot and stood storklike to stub out his cigarette on the boot's sole. He tossed it into the ashtray he'd emptied after lunch. "Chas figures maybe a couple of million folks, you'd be surprised how many gals, are waiting for my latest. Takes me a year, year-and-a-half when research slows me down. Talk Tea Party before I show you what I've penned for the backside of your own book?"

"Oh, sure!"

"Let me get you a drink. Ice water? Sipping whiskey? Got some Dr. Pepper I've been saving."

"What's sipping whiskey?"

"Hundred-eight proof."

"Half that, I think, and half water."

"Carried the barbecue in, figuring rain. Be just a minute turning the ribs, fetching Pussycat her chow. Shall I bring us a plate of oysters and crackers to start?"

"Thanks, no, oysters give me a rash."

"Cottage cheese good?"

"Grand."

In five minutes he approached with a polyethylene bowl. "Sniff."

She complied as thunder sounded.

"Turkey-and-bacon, gourmet for my pal here."

He placed the red bowl next to Pussycat's water dish, disappeared, returned with the tray of drinks and hors d'oeuvres. He hitched up his Levis and settled on a cracked cushion that left another between himself and Jane. "Cheers."

"May we turn on a light?"

"At your pleasure."

Pussycat dipped her muzzle to begin dining. Jane listened to the dog's jaw click, then pulled the chain of a table lamp shaded in vellum, yellowing the darkening room.

"You may know," Mad Dog began, "that Mark Meckler was a punk rock dee jay in LA before moving to the Sierra foothills. That's how he learned that chitchat is what grabs believers. When he and Jenny Beth got together, they applied that technique to social networking on Twitter and Facebook. Plus, naturally, explaining the shame of contraception, and believing it's us children of God that're aggravating global warming.

"Once the Tea Party Patriots reach critical mass here in Santa Fe, I intend—through small talk and anecdotes—to put folks wise to Obama's multiple Social Security numbers and his phony birth certificates. Shall we start with coffee klatches, maybe? Plus notices at the libraries and bookstores—Words, Words, Words; Borders; Hastings; the Ark's too airy-fairy. Grocery bulletin boards? Could be your hubby, being computer-savvy, might lend a hand building us a Web site."

"He doesn't believe in God, Rolf."

"Tempt him, little gal. Wear something off-shoulder."

Jane laughed but Rolf responded with a frown.

"Gonna pitch in?"

"My son, Herk, might help with Internet chores. We could use our home for meet-ups, I suppose. But stop that 'little gal' stuff, will you?"

Jane's eyes misted as she proceeded to tell him about losing Tatum.

"Stupido." He knocked his breastbone with the knuckle of his thumb, then lifted a hip to grab the red, white, and blue neckerchief trailing from a pocket, and handed it across. She patted her eyes while Pussycat padded to the oval throw, and curled beside Jane's feet.

She returned Rolf's neckerchief but had to tug her hand from his grasp. Her stomach started gurgling. To distract him she asked, "Do you make enough from your books to live on?"

"Surely You Jest can be slow with royalties, sure enough." He scratched behind his ear. "Don't really matter, I'm a trust-fund baby. My daddy built offshore oil rigs in Houston, Scotland, Abu Dhabi, Algeria, many places."

"But why do you stay with a local publisher?"

"What about you?"

"We looked hard for New York representation. Couldn't find it."

"Myself, I enjoy role-playing, the cowboy in white that hassles Chas and his better half. The old guy's brainwashed Benji to ape his bullshit that the best life is led without emotion."

"But that's impossible."

"Yep, but he claims Christian Science and its no-emotions claptrap kept him from overdosing on Haldol, I think it was, after finding his long-term playmate—Buck Monk, a heart surgeon here—dead as an overfed bedbug in their Las Campanas hacienda. Dead from stroke. Not right, grown men playing footsie with each other. I suspect the Lord'll take Benji from Chas as well, or vice versa, or both."

"Then they are a gay couple, like my my son said."

"Seems likely, don't it?"

"Benji is what, half Mr. Small's age? You seem so lighthearted about it all."

"The Lord's no doubt Himself laughing. Has a plan, you know that. Smoke!" Rolf pushed himself off the leather cushion. "Gotta transfer those ribs to the oven before they burn. Got some chard from the garden and grits simmering on top. Left your manuscript and my blurb in the kitchen where I do my own first drafts."

"Mine isn't a first draft," Jane called after him, watching his hips swing—why did his body fascinate her so? "Rolf? You've scared me about getting involved with Surely You Jest."

He stopped and turned.

"Are they going to get our book out as fast as Mr. Small claims? Three weeks ago he told me he'd have to publish two books before ours."

"Most of Chas's reasons to sequence certain titles make no sense to me. Be right back."

"Could I have another sipping whiskey?"

"Water?"

She shook her head and leaned down to stroke Pussycat's neck.

After a few minutes, Rolf returned to find Jane holding the shepherd's front paws against her thigh.

"She's been trying to climb up."

"Want me to take her off?"

"We're comfy now."

"Here's your drink."

"None for you?"

"I'll have another with dinner. Let's discuss this blurb thing." He placed the manuscript she'd loaned him on the cushion and, continuing to stand, handed her a sheet of yellow foolscap.

She read the seven lines of script, looked up. "But this will turn readers off."

"Nah, they'll be intrigued. People love to laugh."

"At *we need, indeed, to beautify our homes, replace the locks, so that climate-change thugs will skip our neighborhoods*?" Jane drank half her whiskey. "At *written with a heartwarming earnestness that wouldn't it be some kind of paradise if we all could do as suggested*? You're making fun of Joe and me. This book isn't meant to be a joke."

"Neither is this."

Mad Dog's scarred hands descended to his fly. One grasped his buckle, the fingers of the other tugged on the zipper. He stooped, and after a moment of fiddling, hauled out an erect penis half again the length and girth of Joe's.

"My god!" She leapt up.

Pussycat, ears cocking, rose with her.

"Appreciate the congrats."

"What are you doing?"

The crack of thunder became Jane's starter's gun. She pushed at Rolf's ribcage and he stumbled against a floor lamp, sending it crashing. She dropped the yellow foolscap, snatched up her manuscript and raffia bag, high-stepped over Pussycat's waving tail, hurried toward the front door, flung it open, and ran into an evening shower of hail. The goat, no shelter to trot to, stood roped and bleating.

She tore apart the flaps of her bag and dug for keys. The manuscript slipped from underneath her elbow and fanned into the mud. She bent to gather up the stained pages, tears mixing with what had segued into rain.

"Never meant to offend." Mad Dog shouted from the front porch.

10

Hero

In the news:

Forty U.S. troops, including 22 Navy SEALS and a SEAL dog, plus eight Afghan commandos and an interpreter, died when Taliban terrorists fired on a twin-rotor CH-47 Chinook in mountainous Wardak Province west of Kabal, so far the deadliest incident for U.S. forces in the 10-year Afghanistan war.

For the first time, Standard & Poors plans to downgrade the U.S. credit rating from AAA to AA. Administration officials blamed the setback on flawed analysis after S&P branded Congress as "increasingly dysfunctional, riven by deep partisan divides."

Thirty years have passed since AIDS reared its head in New Mexico. The biggest problem? Public indifference. The tiny red ribbon signifying the fight against AIDS gets lost amid pink ribbons for breast cancer, purple ribbons for domestic violence, and puzzle pieces for autism.

Match.com reports that 17% of couples who married last year met online. If you're hoping to follow suit, be sure to use correct grammar in your first (make it upbeat) e-mail. And never book back-to-back coffee dates—s/he'll suspect you of speed-dating.

No rain for three days; Santa Fe had received less than half the year's norm. On this first Sunday in August, the heat still oppressive at 7 pm, Charlie, Benji, and Benji's mother, Jeannie LaForge, sat on Charlie's back portal spooning up frozen double-fudge yogurt from Charlie's own mother's cut-glass bowls. Short Stuff, Benji's calico, her squirrel-like tail flicking, had been sniffing for lizards under the marigolds bordering the patio wall.

She spotted a black bee buzzing the honeysuckle that Buck Monk— dead now seven years—had planted for hummingbirds at the patio's center. Short Stuff jerked her head left, sounding the bell secured around her neck with red yarn. She dropped her tail and bounded toward the bee. When it flew off, she paraded toward the trio sitting in the overhang's shade.

"More wine? Benjamin, Mr. Small? The shop in Taos is the one place I know outside San Francisco where you can pick up a bottle of Trockenbeerenauslese. It's the only dessert wine I'm aware of, even chilled, that keeps its nose of overripe nectarines. Neither of you has given me your reaction."

"Oh, Mother."

"Well?"

At sixty-one, Jeannie LaForge had a droopier double chin than her son. Otherwise, she looked nearly as trim as he, though she'd found nothing cost-effective to eradicate the wrinkles in her neck.

Since her divorce, she'd worked out faithfully three times a week, first at the gym near her condo in the Oakland Hills, now at Spiritual Fitness, three miles from the earthship she'd purchased a month ago on the flatlands west of Taos. Overeaters Anonymous was keeping Benjamin in good health, at least he'd told her *that* about his life. But why were he and his employer dressed like twins? Were the evening's cargo shorts, sky blue polos, and white socks and white sneakers some kind of summer uniform? Or to demonstrate solidarity at the press?

Benjamin had set up this dinner two weeks ago over the phone, warning her that he'd started gathering his hair into a ponytail. Which is why she had decided for the visit, as a show of unconditional love, to ponytail her own auburn-dyed hair.

She raised plucked brows at him, then at Charlie, and threw her hands out in front of the peasant blouse that she wore above a double-flounced skirt.

"The wine?" Charlie asked. "Yummy, yummy, gimme, gimme." He set the frozen double-fudge on the bench between him and Benji, and extended his goblet.

As the publisher waited for Jeannie to pour, Short Stuff rubbed herself against his sock and rolled to her back to have her tummy scratched. Charlie, however, kicked out, sending the cat skittering.

"Hey, bud!" Benji stabbed his granny glasses to his nose.

Short Stuff's slide stopped near the litter box Benji had placed near the Zuni pot holding trumpets of datura just beginning their evening unfolding.

The goblet of the ultra-sweet, golden nectar sparkled in light about to leave the patio, though the sun would continue for an hour to warm the hacienda and its casita.

Charlie winked at Benji's mother and sipped. "Umm, umm, Jeannie, holy moly matrimony, this wine's delish."

"But that poor cat. Why in the world did you kick her? Thank God she doesn't seem to be limping."

"He hates her," Benji said and upended his glass.

"Cats give me asthma, they shed, they poop. As you can see," Charlie said.

Short Stuff was indeed squatting on her litter, hindquarters vibrating. A dish of food pellets rested beside the box.

"We all 'poop', Mr. Small. Benjamin and I adore cats. Like Zen monks, they rake smooth whatever disturbs them. Do you see that also?"

While Short Stuff pawed litter across her scat, a blue-bellied, whiptail lizard—crimson scar where its tail had been—scampered over the sun-warmed flagstones into the bordering thyme. The calico leapt over the side of her box in pursuit.

Charlie pulled his earlobe, wishing he knew a hex to make this woman cut her visit short. "Possum, hear me clearly!"

"No need to shout, bud."

"I don't care a harem if your mam asked you to bring the cat over. We don't want cats in the office and I don't want them here." He swiveled to face Jeannie. "It's my house until the Possum joins me."

"Joins you?"

"A figure of speech, Mother." How Benji wished the fingers he swung toward her were holding a reefer of marijuana. "Charlie means until I obey orders. A real Nazi, this guy. To whom, let's be real, I owe a good life."

"Go carry that mangy feline and her box and chow inside, boyo, near the fountain. Hop!"

"Mr. Small, I don't like the way you talk to my son. I really don't. And what do you mean by Possum? "

Charlie shrugged and resumed spooning up his double fudge.

"Did you not hear me?"

No response.

Meantime, Benji had tugged Short Stuff backwards out of the flowers, plunked her into her box, and was pulling open the carved door to the great room. Neither noticed the second whiptail, as long as Benji's sneaker, scooting around the corner. It slipped under the skirt of one of two cater-corner sofas near a riff in clear glass of August Rodin's statue, *The Kiss*. Tiles of umber glass covered the encircling ledge. Water dribbled from the lovers' lips into a pool. Benji raised the wall switch that lit the near-replica from inside and cast light up through the pool's bottom tiles.

"Mr. Small?" Jeannie pressed against the wicker chair's back, felt the perspiration that had built, and leaned forward. "One of the reasons I decided to break free and become a poet was that Benji's father wouldn't talk to me. I don't do well with people who can't answer simple questions."

"Preserve us from poets," Charlie muttered as Benji returned and settled beside the datura.

"Perhaps we should be on our way, Benjamin."

"Leave anytime," Charlie said.

"What's the trouble now, Mother?" Beniji flipped his beribboned ponytail to the front of his polo.

"I'm worried about you. I know you'd just as soon not have seen me today—don't say anything—but how I wish you could learn from marital mistakes and marry someone of childbearing age, someone you find more compatible than Marian. I wish I dared show you the poems I've been writing about this."

"Oh, dear bandercock," Charlie wheezed and began twisting his Old Miss class ring.

"You and a new wife should be bringing happiness to children, Benjamin. At least won't you send a card to your fourteen-year-old? Her two younger brothers don't ask yet but Marian says Meadow pleads, 'Why can't I see my dad?'"

"Forget it, Mother. Marian swore she'd not let herself get big-tummied again. The only thing my kids are gonna know about my life is that, thanks to Charlie, their mother receives a monthly cashier's check."

"Atta boyo, Possum."

"His name is Benjamin."

"Calm down, Mother."

"I am calm! I only want you to live a normal life."

Charlie smiled as Benji said, "Don't you know there are no normal lives? Except maybe same-sex couples who've linked up so they won't propel more warm bodies into our clogged-with-people world."

Charlie clapped. "Make sense of that, Benji's mam."

"I can make sense of nothing you or my son say, sir." She grabbed the German dessert wine by its neck and rose. "I'll wait in the car, Benjamin. Your keys, please."

"Didn't lock it."

"Stay a moment, Jeannie. I want to tell you something about my own life. Why do I want to do that? Who knows why but it could be instructive." He placed a liver-spotted hand on her hip.

"Don't touch me!" But she retook her chair and set the bottle back.

"Your idea of normal is wacky-woo. I had to marry twice to find that out."

"Twice?" Benji asked.

"I courted and wed my college's Homecoming Queen, whom my mam had made a fool of herself over. Left her. Then fourteen years ago I felt the stab of love for a woman again, this time for my CPA."

"Kittie?" Benji asked, incredulous.

"Herself. We kept the knot tied for a year. She wanted children, however, and my jism had no bite—embarrassing."

"You seem to scoff at everything," Jeannie said. "What Benjamin's done is no laughing matter. He left someone who still loves him."

"Can't say that about Kittie-poo."

"Marian is raising three children by herself and her stuttering has worsened. She won't date. The only work she's found is indexing for a few textbook publishers in Denver."

Benji found himself wishing that a whiptail—miraculously given a fatal bite—would lunge from the marigolds or thyme or out of the datura to sink its teeth into his mother's ankle.

"I need to reassure you, Jeannie-O, before you and the Possum hightail it out of here, that this Benjamin of yours isn't all bad news. You should see the drop-dead cover he shot a week ago for the most important compendium of tips to save the planet that will see print this year from any press in the country, I feel no doubt. We're sticking our necks out to publish it simultaneously in hardcover, softcover, and as an e-book."

"We are?" asked Benji.

"Didn't I just say so?" Charlie suddenly propelled a hand back over his hair and his face puckered with rage. "Bumblecock and moonshine, people, I own this state's largest commercial publishing company. I have no wil-ly-whompers reason to repeat myself or explain anything. No wonder I lose energy so fast." He snapped off a trumpet of datura and tossed it toward the center bed of honeysuckle. He plucked another blossom, crushed it until its sap trickled down his wrist, and hurled it after the first. When his wheezing had calmed, he hunched his shoulders and said to Benji and his mother, "Am I for real now? I'm trying to explain to both of you how key the press is for getting out world-changing works, like *You Can Save Us All*."

Fearing another outburst, Jeannie said in monotone, "Benjamin told me about the book when he invited me, in your behalf, to drive down to your beautiful home and grounds for dinner."

"Look, I'm a realist, I know the manuscript may have as much effect on mind-sets as expelling a wad of chewing gum into that Zuni pot."

"If I were publisher—"

"Don't push it and someday you will be, boyo."

"Okay. And when I am, I'm gonna have all our authors pay big bucks up front because, you know what? I want to drive a car as humongous as yours."

"Huh? I thought you loved the bumblebee."

"Fitting Mother and Short Stuff and litter and cat food into the Cooper took twenty minutes this afternoon. And the air-conditioner's still busted."

"A CLS-Class, 402-horsepower coupe for the Possum? Wrigglety-piggety, why not? We'll get it painted yellow with black stripes. As well as find you an Armani wardrobe and new furnishings. Though Mary Baker Eddy—"

"Who's Mary Baker Eddy?" Jeannie risked interrupting.

"Thrice-failed spouse and no-way-normal founder of Christian Science, Benji's mam. I'm a church-free Scientist. Mary Baker believed that items like new cars and wardrobes and furnishings are illusory. She served as a medium for the downloading of principles that make the planet spin. The books we publish are testaments to those basics."

"Cut the bullshit, Charlie, okay?"

"No more contradictions, I said!"

"You don't really think our books are important at all," Benji said.

"What in buggeropolis gives you that ill-favored notion?"

"Spirit is immortal truth, books and monster Mercedes and Armani shirts and a mattress I could wake on without a sore back are mortal error, you've drummed that into me, even though..."

"Yes?"

"Forget it."

"We can't follow you, boyo."

"Benjamin," Jeannie said carefully, "I want to do some writing back at the motel. The trout tetrazzini was lovely, Mr. Small, I mean it. Look now how the sun gilds the tops of your quaking aspen. And is that not the whistle of a black-headed grosbeak hidden somewhere? I know it from visits with Marian and the children."

"*Ah, how sweet, how heavenly the sight/ When those who love the Lord/ In one another's peace delight/ and so fulfill His word.* A hymn from my youth, Jeannie. You and your scion need to stay put until we straighten out what I think and what I don't. Mostly I believe *You Can Save Us All* will be as cataclysmic as climate change itself. I also believe that the two books we intend to publish ahead of the how-to-save-our-planet book, if the poets figure out the proper formatting, will be prizewinners on a national scale. Now go home—God bless and good night."

"We're actually publishing the two poetry books, Mother, because we need financial help from one of the authors. The second author is the main author's honey."

While Benji talked, Charlie frowned at his fingernails and rubbed their tips with his thumbs. He then stood without comment, tilted the bowl of melted yogurt into his mouth, wiped his lips with his wrist. "Your wine, madam."

"Please keep it. Oh, dear! Through the window."

Benji rose beside his mother to see Short Stuff on the fountain's tiled ledge confronting the lizard that had lurched inside. Three feet from the cat, on the ledge as well, the lizard was pumping its blue belly up and down. Its own still-attached tail lazed motionless.

Short Stuff pressed her declawed paws against the pool's lip and leapt. The dotted stripes of the whiptail's back vanished as it scurried down the pool's opposite wall. Short Stuff tumbled into the water. The splash, silent to the three watching from outside, created a momentary fountain.

"Can cats swim?" Benji asked, dazed by seeing his calico disappear.

"Of course they can't swim," Charlie said. "Let the damn thing drown."

But he had started running before Benji or his mother could move.

He swung the door to the great room wide. Just inside, a sneaker slipped backward on the Mexican tiling he'd paid a homeless *obrero* to scrub and wax in preparation for Jeannie's visit. He jerked the foot forward in time to regain his balance, hurried to the pool, and stared down into it.

Drops hung like tiny grapes off the calico's white eyebrows. She pawed as though swimming and managed to raise her head. Fur plastered her cheekbones. Her pupils had grown to twice their usual size. She let out a howl.

Charlie bent to lock his hands under her front legs and hoisted her, dripping. But again his foot slipped, then the other. As Short Stuff wriggled from his grasp to clamber onto the encircling ledge, Charlie plunged headlong into the two-feet-deep water.

His eyes and lips clamped shut upon hitting the water's surface and he threw a hand forward to brace his descent. From wrist to elbow burned as though a knife were slitting his right forearm open. He slithered totally under, knowing what that might do to the contents of his wallet, but it seemed the only way to bring his head back into the air. He hauled himself out with his left hand and slumped along the far ledge. His white socks chilled his feet as water continued to gurgle down between the statue's lovers. "Bandercock!" he called out.

The bedraggled cat, her bell soundless, had by now slunk deep into a clump of Apache plume where the patio wall met the house. "C'mon, baby, you're all right," Jeannie coaxed, fisting a couple of red, cotton napkins. "Come to mama, come, baby, let me dry you off."

Benji had raced into the great room. "What happened, bud?" He set his hand on Charlie's shoulder, the polo's sunny blue turned to midnight from the soaking.

"Foolio poontang, oh, lickety-spittle, what's it look like? The sucker hurts; I probably broke my arm. Forget my signing paychecks for a while."

11

Saving Candy

In the news:

Britons in poor communities facing high unemployment, the weak economy, and plunging government funding have lashed out with arson and looting across London and Birmingham. Yesterday rioters set businesses ablaze near the shiny stadiums of next year's Olympic Games.

Bacteria grow fast in the sack lunches of 3- to 5-year-olds, writes dietician Ruth Friendly in the journal, *Pediatrics*. Her study of 705 lunch sacks containing at least one perishable showed only 1.6 percent were stored in lockers located within a safe temperature range.

California felons are using smuggled-in smartphones and Facebook, MySpace, Twitter, and other networking sites to stalk victims and direct outside criminal activities, according to prison officials. Six years ago the department confiscated 261 cell phones compared with 7,284 the first half of this year.

61-year-old marathon swimmer Diana Nyad is attempting to cover the 103 miles from Havana to Key West in an estimated 60 hours. She hopes the effort will improve understanding between Cuba and the United States. Experiencing some asthma, she's swimming without a shark cage.

"Yep," said Benji into the phone two mornings after the Sunday evening spent with his mother at Charlie's. Per Sir Publisher's directive, he'd left Short Stuff at home.

A dusty, two-foot-diameter floor fan swung as he stared at the black-and-white photo in a gold frame perched on the shelf opposite—his father in a Livermore Labs lab coat holding young Benji's hand.

"I'm *sorry*," Benji replied to the husky voice in Amazon's book department. He'd found Amazon's please-rush request curling out of the fax machine fifteen minutes ago. "Rolf Goodenough's *When Wild Bill Spilled Cooper Martin's Blood* has become a best seller for us. Lightning Source can't send out forty copies for two weeks. As a safeguard, shall I double your order to eighty?"

The fan's blades could not keep the sun's heat at bay. Benji pulled a tissue from the box on his desk, wiped his forehead and neck, then stabbed his granny glasses into the bridge of his nose. He jerked sideways to grab Amazon's fax from the side table—causing the ends of the scarlet ribbon securing his ponytail to flop.

"That butterfly lives."

"Huh?" Benji twisted to see Trevor Quesenberry, owner of the bookstore three blocks distant, standing in the doorway dangling an empty carton.

"That's they?" came Charlie's shout from his office across the hall.

"It's Trevor!" Benji called back, then into the phone's receiver, "Apologies. Too much chaos too soon. Good for eighty of the Goodenoughs? Okay, appreciate it."

He placed the order into the wooden tray Candy had lettered *To Do Today* sitting next to the heaped tray, *Forget For Now.*

"What's up, Trevor?" Benji asked.

"Been waiting since seven to get you in here, Possum!" Charlie shouted.

"His Nibs twitchy-squirrelly already?" Trevor's thicket eyebrows lifted under an equally blond roadster cap. He dropped the carton beside a white loafer. "July sales tanked but we're getting mucho requests for your *Tales of Idiots and Madmen: New Mexico's Historic Stopovers.* You've got a dozen copies maybe in the back room so I don't have the vexation of writing something out?"

"Lemme go see."

First Benji peered into Charlie's office. "Finding books for Trevor."

The publisher stared at him between twin monitors and the stack of black-bound *Britannica*s. He took off his reading glasses with his left hand—the ACE elastic bandage that Benji had bought for him yesterday, along with a new wallet, wrapped his right wrist. "Fodder for the fag-o? Tuck your shirt in. Important matter to discuss before the Tashes show up to double my blood pressure."

"Yeah?" Lacking windows, his boss's office smelled mustier even than usual. Perhaps because the fan Benji had bought for him weeks ago sat silent.

"Yeah. Hop, hop."

Benji disappeared and ducked into the mailroom, shelved with Surely You Jest's fastest-moving titles.

Arms laden, he returned to the front office. "Here you go, Trevor." Was the slightly pudgy proprietor of Words, Words, Words experimenting with a peppermint-scented cologne? Benji liked it.

Trevor lifted the empty carton to the counter. "I have to relay this make-your-day tidbit. Yesterday Vanessa What's-Her-Name asked me to ask you or His Nibs if you stock her *Roses and Thorns* in e-book format. 'You mean,' I asked, 'does Surely You Jest store iPads and Kindles in the back room?'"

Chuckling by himself, Trevor said, "Thanks a bunch for these." He stretched to peer over the counter. "Is Charlie-boy also sporting your sockless but nifty blue-and-white athletic shoes and pocketless polos buttoned to the Adam's apple? Of course he is. Bye, bye."

Trevor doffed his cap; blond hair dropped over his ears. He cradled the overflowing carton against a cream-colored blouse and a moment later triggered the front-door's chimes.

When Benji entered Charlie's office, the publisher threw the fingers he'd been examining toward the spindle chair his dead father used to sit straight-backed in for meals. A brass plate, *For Lance Small, Mississippi's Top Ford truck dealer, 1940*, remained tacked to the top crossbar.

"Let's undo top buttons, Possum, what do you say-o? Today's looking to be what my mam called a scorcher."

"Why don't you turn on the fan?"

"With guests coming in, don't like to appear too cheap to buy air-conditioning. Regarding tomorrow: hair-styling day. Candy's off. Let's take the afternoon ourselves, drive over to my place, maybe nap..."

"You never nap."

"By midweek I'm pooped, Possum. We could lounge beside the clubhouse pool."

"I sunburn too easily. And I need to tell you, bud, you were too damned rude to Mother on Sunday."

"You're not thrilled she drove back up to Taos yesterday?"

"What's that have to do with anything? You're rude to everyone, you know that? Why are you short with Candy? She holds this outfit together."

Charlie rose, slapped the desk. "I'm the poontang who saved your cat Sunday! And don't you ever forget who, forty years ago, put this company on its feet. *Charlie Small* is the fella holding this company together. So that someday he can turn it over to you."

"Fine. I'm grateful. But I wish you could shut the hell up sometimes." How he craved a reefer to ignite, his heart was knocking so.

Charlie forced himself not to retort as he slumped back into his swivel chair. He set his chin on his palms, shuddered from the pain that shot to his elbow, and threw the forearm aside. "Kittie called before you showed up. We'll need to file for bankruptcy if we can't replace Sothebys with a major lessee by October. Because I won't try to sell even one of my rental properties. Crack my nuts, Benji, I won't do it.

"So keep doing me small favors like buying me this." He rubbed his palm back and forth along the ACE bandage. "And finding me a new wallet. I'll keep paying for our haircuts And work on my big mouth, okay, Possum?"

They gazed at each other in the wan light the gooseneck on Charlie's desk delivered, listening to the waterworks' clock nearby until the entry chimes rang again.

"Finally." Charlie reached into a drawer. "Joe and Jane Tash. Their text CD needs an overhaul."

Benji hurried out.

It was Herk, however, taller than Charlie remembered, who appeared first, black-and-white sneakers squeaking. Dressed in the black tee and silver-buckled shorts Charlie recalled from the pork's last visit, Jane's son gave him a one-sided smile.

Charlie gestured at the sofa fronting the wall of titles displayed face out: southwestern history, travel guides, shoot-em-up novels, poetry.

"Here?" Herk asked.

"Got a good reason why not?"

Jane followed with her briefcase. The auburn hair she mostly wore in a twist lay knotted this morning on top of her head, making her almost Herk's height. A shirtdress bowed at the small of her back matched the clip holding her hair.

Herk settled his Stetson on his knees. "Your show," he told his mother.

"So where's Joe?" Charlie pinched up the CD holding the text of *You Can Save Us All* that Herk had brought Benji on Friday.

"Every specialist he's seen," Jane said, pulling the dress tight under her buttocks before descending next to Herk, "seems to have a different opinion. One gastroenterologist suggested him undergoing on the same day an endoscopy down the throat and colonoscopy up his bum. Last week a neurologist told him to visit a certain psycho-, psycho-, *psychophysiologist* who focuses on belly cramps that have no physical cause. The bunion of Joe's left foot hurts him, too, worse and worse. And his back."

Charlie stared at her.

"What happened to your arm? Bar fight?" Herk asked.

Refusing to respond, Charlie wriggled the CD at Jane. "I have some bad news. This has to be redone before I can e-mail edited text back to you and your husband, get your sign-offs, and turn it over to our art director to choose typefaces and font sizes. She'll come up with a book design and e-mail the files to our printer in Nashville."

"But what if—"

Charlie held up his palm. "I've put aside an hour for us to go over the *Author's Guide* now. We won't need your son, by the way."

"But Herk drove."

"Lots of galleries near us, and until they open, Starbucks is just off the Plaza."

"I don't leave Mom alone with you."

"Good dog," Charlie blurted.

"Herk, baby?"

"I don't trust him."

"Oh, darn it all, you two!" Jane knuckled the side of her thigh. "Herk, leave."

"No."

"Then I'll ask my three questions anyhow. Mr. Small, I need reassurance. Do you still believe our book is important?"

"Absolutely and why I'm giving you, let's see, fifty-five minutes now."

"Do you really intend not to publish it until you've gotten out the two poetry books you talked about at our cover shoot?"

"That's correct."

"Why?"

"Mumbledee bandersnatch, lady, not your concern." Charlie felt sweat dampening his polo. And what kind of perfume was that filling his office? Night-blooming snakeweed? "Achoo!" he exploded, brought the bandaged forearm across his nostrils, and began to wheeze.

Jane waited for a second sneeze that didn't come. "All right, third question."

First he blew into a handkerchief. "The clock's ticking."

"If early next week we can get you a CD that suits you, all right if it doesn't contain both back-cover blurbs? You've seen Lester Brown's—"

"Sorry, didn't notice."

"It's on the CD but I don't feel right in rushing Marta Means. She asked an hour ago while we were climbing into Herk's truck if I could give her a week."

"Blurbs don't sell books."

"When we first met, you implied they do."

"Oh? Yes? Don't believe everything I say. Forget blurbs, hire a professional reviewer to place raves on Amazon, Twitter, Facebook, LinkedIn, whatever. That's today's way to sell books, Benji tells me. Plus schedule readings. And take comp copies to publications here in Santa Fe as well as cities you tour. We're going to gift you with an eight-hundred-page handbook that explains tons of gimmicks that maximize sales. Blurbs maximize nada."

Suddenly: "Charlie!"

He raised his eyes to see Candy holding the doorknob.

"I'm in conference, can't you see?"

She smoothed her hands down her leather skirt. "I'm hurting, Charlie. May we go into the hall? It won't take a minute. Please?

"Mea culpa," she told Herk and Jane, raising her hands to cup her breasts, hidden under a purple tunic. One of her clogs knocked the jamb as she wheeled and left the door wide.

Charlie backed his chair toward the windowless wall. "I'd better see what in cockamamie hell the problem is. Don't move."

They heard his "Benji! Coffee for our guests!" after he shut the door.

When he began shouting again, Herk jumped up, swung the door inward, and dashed out to see Candy flattening palms and shoulders against the hall's far wall. "Benji," she was crying out, "help me!"

Charlie had vised her elbow but Herk, towering over the publisher, shoved him into the wall. "Watch the bad arm, Pork." For protection, Charlie wedged it between his own hip and Candy's.

Benji, who'd been on the phone, came rushing out. "What happened?" He paused a few yards away.

Candy raised her head. "I promised Leonard I'd give notice today and while working on the cover for Sabatini's poetry, I found the nerve."

Charlie looked up at Herk. "Let me loose, I'm warning you!"

"The pleasure's mine, fruitcake." Herk pounded the publisher's shoulders to the stucco, backed away, stepped to Candy's other side, and turned.

"I think you've hurt him," she said.

"Fiddlefart hurt me is right." Sniffing up phlegm, Charlie moved elbows and shoulders in a cautious circle. "Am I going to press charges? Maybe, you bet. But I suspect this publishing deal with your betters is right now hurtling like the passenger pigeon into oblivion."

"I promised my husband to quit because of Charlie's tantrums," Candy told Herk.

"Tantrums?" Charlie said. "So far you've seen zip, believe me, toots."

"What's this 'toots,' bud?" But Benji did not budge from his safe distance.

"Your raging, your awful silences, and the workload you expect. It's not fair. All I do at night is cry, Charlie. Criminy, I've started crying Sunday afternoons at my piano lesson."

"You're plucking my heartstrings," the older man said.

"I didn't want to burst in on your meeting. But Leonard says he can't take it anymore. Last night he told me to choose between him and you."

She glanced up at Herk but he had fixed Charlie with his gaze, pushing his jaw forward in a sawing motion as though waiting to punch him out.

"Of course I had to give notice. When Leonard and I married we signed a prenuptial agreement. What would I live on?"

"Spare me the melodramatics, okay?"

"I don't want to quit."

"Of course you don't want to quit."

"Especially before I finish the Tashes' project. Herk has some lovely design ideas."

"Publishers..." Benji began, hoping to play peacemaker, wishing Marta were here to do it more effectively. How would she handle this?

The phone started in again. Too much to do, too much. But Benji stepped forward and summoned the words Charlie had made him get by rote three months into this job. "Publishers are sure of their intuitions and instincts while authors are wanderers with no belief systems. Except, of course, you," Benji improvised for Herk. "And folks like your mother and your dad."

"I'm no author and Joe's not my father, pint-size," Herk said. "I grew up peeking at him from outside the back-porch window fucking women he'd brought home"—Herk circled Candy's shoulder—"sorry, but fucking's the word. Drunk out of their skulls. In front of my mother, who was afraid to run. That's the woman sitting in your boss's office right now. Okay, sport?"

Candy, Benji, and Charlie stood silent until finally Benji wet his lips. "We at Surely You Jest are doing the right kind of work in the right place. By envisioning a random field of blossoms arranging themselves into different patterns, each day we know what to do. Mary Baker Eddy gives us principles. Though we are strengthened by her knowledge of perfection, we live a life of surprises. Our particular skill is dropping sand into an oyster and opening the shell to discover a pearl."

"Are you two dudes nutso? Candy, quit, for God's sake." Herk wheeled, opened the door to Charlie's office, and ran to his mother. He snatched up her briefcase, then, by her elbow, her. "There must be other publishers in Santa Fe. Or we'll sign on with Lulu or CreateSpace to help you and Joe get your dreamy-eyed manuscript into print. But promise me you'll break your contract here. These guys are kooks, Mom."

"Mr. Small has the CD."

"No, there it is, tossed on the table with head shots of his supposedly best-selling authors."

Benji had vanished when Herk led Jane into the hall. They spotted Charlie's rump disappearing into the restroom.

Candy sat pressing her temples on the bench intended for visitors. "Oh, drat," she said, looking up. She rose. "What a mess I've made."

"Wrong. You were beautiful." Herk hugged her against his ribs until she ducked and backed away. "I've got to get to work, tomorrow's my day off. I'll probably spend the whole thing under the covers."

"Let's do it together."

"Herk!" his mother exclaimed.

But Candy laughed, turned, and clicked down the hall. They waited to head for Herk's truck until her door slapped shut.

Having pooped, peed, and re-combed his hair, Charlie marched into Benji's office. "Don't answer if the phone jangles—it's sharing time." He took a chair to the side of the swinging fan. "Stop shuffling those orders or return-for-credit vouchers or whatever. And stop trying to protect Candy. That's this poontang's job until my mortal coil waves bye-bye to this error-ridden world. Candy's not going to resign, I'll see to that in a moment."

"Exactly how?"

"Money talks."

"I thought we were going bankrupt."

"*To those leaning on the sustaining infinite, today is big with blessing.* Have particular faith in Seńor Sabatini, boyo. Infinite Mind tells me he's going to come through. More important is this. At Pranzo's three weeks ago you got sore in the parking lot and snapped my suspenders. 'Quit fooling around with women, mister,' I remember is what you said. 'I need a committed relationship.' You recall?"

"Of course."

"Don't you think I need that, too, Possum? You stay away from Candy. I don't even any longer want you fixing her coffee. Got it?"

Charlie gazed across until Benji dropped his eyes.

"I got it," he whispered and raised them again. "Can't we work something out with Short Stuff? Like maybe come with me here every other day?"

"Tomorrow we leave for the stylist's before noon."

"Day after, then?"

The phone rang.

"Better take that. I'll go butter up Candy."

12

Wrong

In the news:

Democrat Jerome Block Jr.'s four fellow Public Regulation Commissioners have asked him to vacate the $90,000-a-year position following allegations of auto theft, absenteeism, and campaign-fund and gasoline-card misuse.

Guadalupe Padilla and Sharon Baca have been arrested for fifteen residential burglaries. Alex Chavez has been arrested for hiding in the ceiling of his pizza parlor —pending resale— their stolen TVs, DVD and MP3 players, computers, and video-game systems.

The 55-year-old head of the Fundamentalist Church of Jesus Christ of Latter Day Saints in Texas has been handed a life sentence for collecting 24 child brides to please him sexually, citing God's will in thousands of pages he wrote out in long-hand with a Biblical flourish.

Cookbook authors Bruce Weinstein and Mark Scarbrough explain why, despite being the most popular red meat in the world, Americans eschew goat: "Goat doesn't lend itself easily to factory farming, so it can't be mass-produced."

"**W**hat's wrong?" Joe asked at six the following evening. "I'll tell you what's wrong. You're wrong. Oh, shit, I'm sorry, Jane, this project's going to see me permanently in bed with colonic cramps."

Though he'd given up swimming at his club in New York after Tatum's death, because of today's lingering heat he sat shirtless in red bathing trunks and flip-flops under a fan in the breakfast nook.

He arched backward until his shoulder blades met the chair's top, then reached around and down, hoping to relieve the pain at the base of his spine.

"Tuscan poppies?" he exclaimed, and batted the basketful of papier-mâché blossoms to the edge of the glass-topped table, where half spilled onto the floor. "They're as wrong for New Mexico as you and I are wrong—for each other, Jane! What was the crushing of our little girl but a large white flag flapping over our marriage? Oh, what am I saying? It's this book that's driving me nuts."

He rose, wobbling as a spasm threw another knife into his gut, and lurched toward her.

She stood at the stove, poised to carry a steaming pot of pinto beans to the sink, and flinched when he wrapped an arm around her tummy from behind. Hot water and a handful of beans leapt out and landed on her sandal.

"That hurts! Let go!" She set the pot on the counter and bent.

"What hurts?"

"What do you think? You hurt. The top of my foot hurts. Get away."

"Look, I apologize. I'm sorry." He stumbled back to his chair.

Beyond the door to a rear patio, the tips of cottonwood branches fluttered in the breeze as a mountain chickadee repeated its high, brief song, "Feebee, feebee." Cicadas were buzzing in the potted junipers—and seventy-five yards to the south, beside the stile Herk had built for Marta, her piebald mare whinnied for its oats.

Meanwhile, a quarter mile upstream, Herk had spread the legs of his easel on Little Tesuque Creek.

Jane slipped her right foot from its sandal and brought the sponge down to wipe it clean. With Joe so on edge, she determined to speak carefully. She bought time by opening a door to the oak-clad Sub Zero, extracted a plate of spinach quiche bought at Saveur in Santa Fe, and set it beside the pot of beans. "Babe? Herk says he'll help us self-publish the manuscript, using a website he knows about."

"You told me that yesterday."

"I just want to relieve the pressure you're feeling."

"And how are we supposed to promote the thing?"

"Same as if we stay with Surely You Jest. This book is God's will. I felt it again when Herk and I were at Holy Faith on Sunday. I know you don't believe me and I don't care. The work has kept us going, hasn't it?"

"And you're saying restart the whole formatting process from scratch by self-publishing?"

"Herk understands how."

"I can't work with your son, you know that."

"All right, then, we stay with Mr. Small. If the art director sticks around and he'll still have us."

"You don't care if he's gay?"

"Sure I care but so what? The priest at Holy Faith is gay. And you did spend yesterday afternoon and this morning pouring over the *Authors' Guidelines*, redoing the CD. Let's keep to the plan we came up with at lunch. I'll bring the disk to Mr. Small tomorrow, late morning, even if I can't get an appointment. I'll try to secure his promise to approve galleys by a certain date and set the publication date so we can begin booking readings, starting at the bookstore down from his building. This is all so exhausting, Joe."

Jane settled on the stool Herk had painted with mustard blossoms. They'd bought it at the Shidoni Gallery soon after moving from Connecticut seven months ago. Sweat cooled Jane's buttocks as they pressed her shorts to the cushion. She undid two buttons of her shirt and fanned its collar's flaps across her bra as, suddenly dreading Joe's response, she watched him stand.

He paced between the table's end and the back door, saying nothing for a long minute, then:

"If it weren't for this project, we, at least I, would be heading on home."

"What do you mean?"

"This morning Howard fired off an e-mail asking if I'd consider taking over the Commodities Department again at Goldman."

Goosebumps iced the forearms she'd crossed.

Joe continued to pace, high-stepping over the fallen, faux poppies. "Health services in the City Different are childlike. Last week when the X-ray machine broke down? Before my endoscopy? Before I had to take off my gown, reschedule for another thirty-mile round-trip Friday? The aide gave me a five-dollar coupon for lunch in the cafeteria."

"You didn't tell me."

"Haven't told you this, either. Our personal investments are tanking—I'm no work-at-home trader. At least in REITs or bonds or securities. Pork bellies I know, orange juice, poultry, precious metals, soybeans. But our holdings in Eastman Kodak, in Research in Motion, BankAmerica—"

"All *right*, Joe. You've made your point. You want to move back east, even though Herk and I love it here, though making friends at church is taking more time than I'm used to. What are you suggesting? A week-ends-only relationship? We started *You Can Save Us All* to re-glue the two of us. And we've come to believe the book can be a force for good worldwide. I still do, anyhow. Herk never has. Now you don't?"

"Chapters six through nine are plain stupid. No wonder we couldn't find a New York agent. "

Jane began to snuffle. "How are they stupid, Mister Know-It-All?"

"Let's Tend Our Gardens? Let's Beautify Our Homes? Dressing to Give Pleasure? Cooking Our Way to Serenity? These are going to save the world from disaster? That's goddamn ridiculous; I need a smoke." Joe reached bare-armed for the Baggie he'd set on a windowsill, pried it wide, yanked out a strip of jerky, popped it into his mouth.

Jane grabbed her throat and began to dry-heave. She swallowed and brushed some hair off her eyes. "Not a bit ridiculous. This stuff we worked hard on *together*, you bastard. God won't put up with you, Joe, you'll see."

She jumped off the stool, grabbed a handful of cooling beans from the water, ran over, and mashed them against his scalp. "You cannot do this to our marriage. You can't work with Herk? I can't work with *you*."

The wind chimes she'd had Herk install beside the front door rang out. As Joe scraped the mess from the top of his head, neck, and chest, shaking it from his palm onto the center of the table, Jane rushed into the great room, where she opened to their neighbor. "Oh, darling!"

Dressed in riding boots, jodhpurs, and a tank top, and smelling sweetly of oats, Marta Means let Jane wrap her shoulders with both bean-smeared hands.

"What am I interrupting?" Jane's neighbor asked in her six-years-past-smoking rasp. She stared into her friend's bleared eyes.

Jane drew back, took one of Marta's hands. "Not dinner, that's ruined except for the quiche." She saw that the other hand held a shopping bag lettered *Tesuque Market*.

Marta's eyebrows gathered. "I felt bad telling you that I needed a week to pen a blurb for your back cover. So I've got it on a CD, burned just now after feeding the mares. It's in the bag with your manuscript. What a fabulous read, Jane! You and Joe have got here a major accomplishment and we all should be grateful. So many good ideas.

"And guess what? Greta and Philippe have accepted our offer. They move into the apartment over my garage Saturday the twentieth—Indian

Market weekend—and begin gardening and housekeeping for us. Greta even says she'll cook for an extra two hundred a month."

"I'm so glad but look, oh, God, I'm weeping again. Mr. Small as much as threw Herk and me out of the office yesterday."

"Why? Charles's rages are getting to be horribly inappropriate."

Jane ran a fist along the washed-this-morning twist of hair hanging down her chest. "My son felt Mr. Small was abusing the art director. She'd threatened to quit."

"Do you blame her?"

"I'm so muddled, Marta. Herk has asked me to break our contract. Unless Mr. Small breaks it first. Fifteen minutes ago Joe called the book silly and told me I'm-not-sure-what about our marriage. He *was* clear that he wants to return to working in New York." She wiped her eyes with the back of a hand and dried it on her apron.

Marta set her shopping bag onto the foyer's pavers and gripped Jane's upper arm. "You leave Charles and Herk to me. Joe's more a handful. Come along. Let's see how he's feeling now."

Marta picked up the bag and led the way over the Navajo carpet that softened a third of the great-room's Mexican tiles. Past leather armchairs and a custom-built armoire, the women entered the dining room, where a chandelier of elk horns dominated the table. They stopped at the arch separating dining room and kitchen.

Joe, back at the breakfast nook's table, had cleaned it of beans. The fan above him had begun to squeak, sounding like the chickadee in the cottonwood. To Jane his head seemed a bent sunflower gone to seed.

He raised his eyes. "Holding hands? You two getting cozy? My own life's over, kaput. Okay, Jane? Happy?"

"Snap out of it, Joseph." Marta moved ahead of Jane, stopped beside the toaster oven, dropped the paper bag, vised her hips, and thrust her over-sized breasts at him.

A mythical Mayan princess, Jane thought.

"You leave this lady alone," Marta said. "Do you know what a force for good she is? How important *you* are? To her, to your stepson, to me, to everyone who reads this *masterpiece*." She grabbed up the bag and rattled it. One of the paper handles tore loose but she gave it two more shakes. "I'm *ashamed* of you, sir, frightening this sweetheart, threatening to skedaddle back east before you start your readings." Marta wagged a ringed forefinger at him. "For shame, Joseph!"

"What, what? Get the hell out of here. Get this lesbo out, Jane, before I lose it."

"How dare you call our neighbor names."

"I'll say whatever I like."

"Oh, no." Jane darted to a spot beside Marta.

"Say what I like and take action when I like."

"Not while I'm around," Marta said.

"But you're going to go poof in a moment." Joe picked up the fork beside the napkin Jane had set for dinner. He spit the fatty residue from the jerky onto his place mat and started toward his wife and Marta, small eyes nearly closed.

He stopped at the sound of gravel crunching as Herk's red pickup came curving up the drive.

13

What's God's Will?

In the news:

Fifty-nine-year-old Ernesto Baca delivered a blow to the head of 39-year-old Sebastian Gordon on August third. Gordon died at Christus St. Vincent Regional Medical Center a week later. Baca claimed self-defense, explaining he'd refused to buy a coral-studded bracelet Gordon had offered him.

At least 400 students, teachers, and parents cooked in the open and thus ate contaminated rice balls at Karino Elementary, six miles from the March 11 earthquake-and-tsunami-hit Fukushima Daiichi nuclear plant. Warnings they would be in the path of the deadly plume never reached them.

Last night the following items, among dozens of others, were stolen, police reported, from Santa Fe homes: a closet's worth of clothing, seven rings, $12,000 worth of silverware, a flat-screen TV, an iPad, a Dell computer, a stereo, and 60 compact disks.

Letter to the Editor: You're politically incorrect, Patrick Lannan. Since 1998, when you started bringing in writers and activists to lecture on human rights for your foundation, only 29 percent have been women. Yet we gals ultimately have been the world's greater influence for good.

At three o'clock the next afternoon, though the temperature held at close to ninety, rain drummed the hoods of cars and three pickups parked in the Words, Words, Words shared lot.

Jane Tash opened the door of her Honda Civic, shouldered her bag, extended and unfurled her umbrella to shield her briefcase, and—as drops splashed her wrists—dashed into the bookstore, wondering if Marta had arrived early.

They'd agreed to meet over scones after Jane had talked with the store's owner. For the attempt to secure a reading date, she'd chosen to wear what Joe named this morning as her most alluring outfit, a sleeveless, light-gray frock imprinted with honeysuckle blossoms.

She shook the rain from her umbrella and scanned the room; it smelled deliciously of coffee brewing. Thanks to the ceiling's acoustical tiling, talk was so low that she could hear cooled air droning out from vents. Only a man with a turkey feather in his hat and a newspaper on his lap occupied facing sofas. No one stood beside the fireplace nor the rounder holding children's books.

The rows of folding chairs fronting a wooden platform signaled a reading tonight, she decided, and her heart, as though zapped by a pacemaker, speeded its beat. Two couples, one holding hands, sat gazing at the photos of local authors that graced the orange wall behind the microphone. Her eyes caught the back of a leather vest worn over a red-and-blue-checked shirt. The boots, the tattered hat—Rolf, standing at the huge bulletin board taking up a third of another wall.

Jane twisted her head to focus on the counter and its registers. It stretched from the coffeemakers and deli case to the store's main entrance on Water Street. Customers lined up at a register behind which stood, based on Marta's description, Trevor Quesenberry—a bit pudgy, sleeves of a creamy blouse rolled to the elbows, yellow neckerchief.

Unless Marta was in the restroom, she'd not arrived. Jane seesawed her lips to smooth the gloss, and stumbled, flipping a corner of the tasseled throw rug displaying the caves at Chaco Canyon. She caught her balance in time not to fall, and called to a clerk about her age who wore a lap apron declaring, *Words, Words, Words/like Desert Showers*. She'd just straightened from moving books from a cart onto shelves headlined, *This Year's* Times' *Best Sellers*.

"Is that the store's owner?" Jane pointed.

"Yep, Trevor, filling in. We're short this afternoon."

Jane had washed her hair and, with Joe's grunted assent, left it loose for storming the Surely You Jest gates this morning. Shaking her umbrella once more, she furled and telescoped it to fit her bag. She hurried past the rack of travel guides, then the pastries set on paper doilies, to the first register, an antique with a pull-down lever. Silver filigreed its sides. Jane smiled at Trevor over the head of a girl in short shorts and halter who handed him a book and twenty-dollar bill. The graying hair falling over his ears flopped as he rang her up. The girl took her book and change, swayed rather than walked toward the exit, because of roller skates, Jane realized.

"Trevor?"

"At your service."

"I'm Jane Tash. Charles Small at Surely You Jest asked me to schedule a reading if possible. Mr. Small will be publishing my husband and me soon. Hardcover and softcover and e-book all at once."

"Oh? What's the title—excuse me. This wretched day."

He reached to stop the phone from ringing. "Trevor Quesenberry. Words, Words, Words. So glorious here in Santa Fe. May I be of service?

"Jacky! You're calling from the back of a cab? Steaming hot in New York? You'll have to shout, Jack."

Jane stared fascinated at Trevor's nostrils flaring. His thicket brows rose.

"But, Jack, I've got an intern drafting the store's ad right now for our newspaper's arts supplement. Oh—I'm truly sorry your wife feels that way. Yes, sure. And bye-bye to you, Jacky."

The owner's fleshy face had reddened. "Major cancellation. Jack McCready's neighbor in New Haven told Jack's wife that this store loves coming-out readings for lesbians and gays. Yes, we *are* pansexual, no discrimination except against pedophiles. You've got a gay parrot who's dictated a book? Lordy, of course we'll publicize it."

"May we talk now?"

"I've got to stop publicity on Jackoff's political thriller. Meet me in ten minutes by the sofas, all righty?"

Okay, Jane decided, I'll go say hi to Rolf. She passed *Poetry* and *Creative Nonfiction* to come up behind him, shutting her eyes against the lure of jeans that seemed so customized to fit. A smoky scent wafted off his shirt.

"Hello, there," she said softly.

He lowered the notice he'd been positioning against the dark cork, stepped to the side, and gazed down at her. The corners of his light blue eyes crinkled. "Hello yourself. No hard feelings, ma'am?"

"Don't we know each other better than 'ma'am'?"

"Jane, then."

"What've you got there?"

The pale yellow of Rolf's broadside matched the blossoms on her dress:

Let's Cut Government Down to Size.
Tea Party Patriots Call Global Warming Flimflam, Want Climate Change in Politics
Obamacare, Goodbye
Let's Give Santa Fe Its First Sane PAC
Come Gather Round on Thursday, August 25, at 7 pm. For directions call Rolf Goodenough at 505/473-4957
Free Tricorns   Hand-Painted Patriotic Pins
Fifteen Million Believers Can't Be Wrong

"Be downright tickled if you showed up for this, my spread." Rolf doffed his hat, bit into its rim, spit a splinter of straw onto the floor.

"Where are you getting the hand-painted pins?"

"Son Greg found a supplier of blanks in Chattanooga. Talked his pals at Baptist into doing the enameling. He's flying home for the meet-up. Good chance for you and him to say howdy."

"I suspect I'll pass, Rolf, given what happened a week ago, though I've told no one, nor intend to."

"Nothing happened, Jane. You with me? This old coot forgot his manners. What're you up to here?"

"Hope to schedule a reading with Mr. Quesenberry for the book."

"You still want yourself a blurb? I'll write you a crackerjack, Scout's honor." He slapped his vest.

"Oh, Rolf. Marta Means, our neighbor—you met her at the shoot—has brought Joe and me a very nice blurb."

"Glad all's well. I need to get this notice up. Serious business, not a joke."

Wasn't "not a joke" exactly what she'd said to him a week ago about *You Can Save Us All* before he unzipped his fly? The phrase some kind of sexual open sesame? Seeing his fingers descend, she spun around.

Her shin barked a leg of the rostrum displaying Webster's *Third New International.* She stumbled against a corner of the reading platform and crumpled to the parquet as pain shot up her calf. Moaning, she drew her knees to the raffia shoulder bag lying aslant her belly.

"Sweetheart!"

Deep cleavage and the smell of oats greeted her as Marta bent to slip fingers beneath her shoulders. Black curls tumbled from under Marta's wide ribbon, tickling Jane's face. "Let me help you to a sofa."

"I'm not sure I can walk."

"Let's try."

To secure it, Marta pushed the strap of Jane's shoulder bag closer to Jane's neck, and picked up the briefcase.

With her Tesuque neighbor's help, she limped to the nearer sofa and sat.

Rolf rushed over, his face impassive.

A few customers gathered. A woman pushed the spine of a boy wearing a cap on backwards. "Go get her a glass of water."

Trevor shoved his way through and knelt. "Shall I summon an ambulance?"

"I think I'm okay." Jane grasped Marta's hand and the PhD, smoothing her leather skirt with her free hand, settled on a twin cushion.

"Give me another ten minutes, can you?" asked Trevor, rising. "The beautiful anthropologist is taking good care?"

When Jane nodded, he rushed off, loafers slapping the parquet until he reached the lightning bolts and ponies with which most of the store was carpeted.

"Ma'am—Jane," Rolf said. "Got the notice tacked up but I'm thinking it best to hang around. Nothing pressing back home, Pussycat and the livestock don't get their feed until later. You may need some assistance if this other one isn't able, begging your pardon, ma'am." Mad Dog swept his hat toward Marta and bowed.

"No need, Rolf, I have my car."

"If you can't drive?"

"Take a hint, buster!" Marta blurted. "The girl wants you gone."

"Got some reading to do." Rolf turned on his boot heel, moseyed along the coffee table until he reached the opposite sofa. He picked up *Wild Mustangs* among a display of photography books and sat.

The capped boy, cuffs dragging, gave the full glass he gripped to the woman who'd sent him. "Water," she said to Jane and placed it on the table. "Now we'll find your book on magic tricks," she told the boy and headed toward the *How-To* shelves.

Jane started to massage her knee but Marta set the hand back in Jane's lap and substituted both of her own. "You rest. I'm wondering, should I drive you to the ER?"

"Joe's had such disappointments at St. Vincent, I'd rather take my chances."

Marta stopped kneading. "I'll go fetch us coffee. You need something stronger than water."

After she left, Rolf sauntered over. "I wanted to explain."

"Won't you just go?"

"You saw me reaching down for thumbtacks, missy."

"Thumbtacks?"

"Is this what scared you?" Rolf dropped his hand. The cracked nails shone under the fluorescents.

"Don't! Please!"

"Thumbtacks, you see?" From his pocket he extracted a Baggie holding twenty red-, yellow-, and silver-headed tacks. "Couldn't find none loose on the corkboard."

Jane spoke past three fingers she'd pushed against her lips. "Oh, Rolf, I'm so sorry. I thought—"

He raised a hand to stop her. "Your friend's coming. But you and I have made peace, yes? Shake on it?"

She took his hand but recoiled as she felt his squeeze.

Marta cleared a corner of the table for the coffee steaming in Styrofoam and two paper plates holding scones. "Jane told you to scram," she rasped, and recommenced rubbing Jane's knee.

"Rolf, take half of this, will you?" Jane leaned forward to break her scone in two, kept part, lifted the plate.

"Appreciate it." He carried the offering to the cushion on her other side and settled himself. "Major force for good, us Surely You Jest authors. Natural sidekicks." He bit into his scone and swept the crumbs off his thigh.

"But you two want to talk and I'm intruding. Rolf, compadre, bite the bullet." He jumped up, fluttered his sombrero at them, and headed for the arched door.

"He and I each lost a daughter, Marta. And have shared political beliefs. I feel somehow motherly toward the guy. Too strange."

"What happened to you at the publishers this morning?" Marta broke off a corner of pastry, pushed it between her lips, extended her tongue to lick her fingertips.

"The art director was pulling out of her space when I arrived, and Benji and Mr. Small were about to follow. Off to lunch. He started to get upset that I had no appointment but Benji calmed him enough that I was able to secure a commitment—*shamed* him, Marta, frankly—to rush galleys for Joe or me to pick up no later than Tuesday, even though he grumped he'd have to work this weekend."

"That's Charles shamming. He and Benji slave seven days a week." Marta sipped her coffee, focused again on Jane's knee.

Jane let her cup cool. "I got a let's-shoot-for-publication date the second Monday of next month if Joe and I can turn galleys around in forty-eight hours."

"Well, nice going, you." Marta stopped rubbing long enough to grip Jane's shoulder and shake it.

"Your massaging worked wonders, Marta, you see?" Jane lifted her foot straight up, lowered it. "Wonder if I can stand." She did so, returned to the cushion. "Dear Marta, I'm so grateful for your friendship. And so confused! I watch my opinion of what's true and good change second by second. Am I just a concept I've created to push a book that I've thought, with God's help, could save our planet from annihilation? Or is annihilation what our Creator and His Son want? Or am I simply one-hundred-percent misguided about what their will for us human beings is?

"I say Joe's mostly to blame for how I feel but maybe not. He's so unhappy away from the east coast, and starting to undermine all the effort we've put into the manuscript. Especially the later chapters, how glamorizing our meals, our homes, our gardens—ourselves—can give such a powerful boost to the love people can show toward their world."

"But of course Joe would malign those chapters," Marta said. "There's no machismo in them."

"I don't want to lose him!" Jane threw her face to her neighbor's bosom and Marta, warming, wrapped an arm around her.

Trevor, greeting customers, waved at the two new friends as he hurried close. "Thanks a bunch for waiting. Her I know. And you're whom again?"

"Jane Tash, you big teddy, and a powerful writer Charles has discovered. Her book is *You Can Save Us All*, a practical guide for rescuing the earth, a fresh approach. Here's the text. I'm supplying one of her back-cover blurbs." Marta unsnapped the flaps of Jane's briefcase, extracted the just-shy-of four-hundred, double-space pages, and handed the sheaf to Jane. "I'll let her tell you."

Trevor extended his chubby fingers toward Jane. "Keep the text. Might you have books in three weeks?"

"Mr. Small told me *yes* this morning." The storeowner's peppermint scent seemed stronger than when they'd met, but Jane succeeded in stifling a sneeze.

"If our gorgeous hussy vouches the story's good—"

"Knock it off, Trevor. Nonfiction. A blockbuster."

"Then let's fill the slot just vacated by our henpecked New Yorker, Jacky, else you'll have to wait until late October." Trevor took a notepad from his pocket and uncapped his golden fountain pen. "Friday, September thirty, six pm, day after Rosh Hashanah. Even though it may be freezing, the galleries are open late, people are out. We'll contact *Pasatiempo* and get you into our e-mailed newsletter. You might want to hire a book reviewer off the Web as well."

"Jane, write down the reading date on the top page of your text."

"Bossy, bossy," Trevor told Marta.

"And I'm going to be twisting your arm after New Year's for my own two hours of limelight from a sizzling-hot memoir cobbled from my preteen years," she said.

"Doll spills all?"

"In unexpected ways. And heroic—why I'm rendering the revelations into pentameter couplets."

Trevor tinkled more than laughed, then addressed Jane. "You said yours will be an e-book as well as hardback?"

She nodded, adding, "Softcover, too."

"Lots of promotion possibilities. We'll get you onto our e-book link, compatible with all devices except Kindle. We'll offer the e-books at the same price as your paperback. I urge you to set up a website and a blog, and to create a presence on LinkedIn, Twitter, and Facebook."

"I'm going to need to prod Charles to hustle on production," Marta said.

"If my husband and son will pitch in, we can do it." Jane's forearms and chest buzzed with excitement.

"I want you to call the store tomorrow after ten and talk ASAP with Dana Lessering, our intern. She'll detail what we need from you and what *you* can do to maximize crowd size."

Becoming light-headed, Jane took Marta's arm. "I'll call her tomorrow, a promise."

"All righty." The bottoms of Trevor's slacks spread like spinnakers as he moved past the rounder of travel guides toward the registers.

"Let's make sure you can walk." Marta helped Jane rise, then bent to stuff the manuscript into the briefcase. She left the flaps unsnapped, fit the strap of the raffia bag over Jane's shoulder, and handed her the briefcase.

When they reached the door to the lot, Marta stepped ahead and pulled it open. The boom of thunder greeted them but the rain had already become drizzle. Sunshine lit the ski slopes fifteen miles distant, coloring them a ripe peach.

Before passing down the two steps, Marta turned, pressed Jane's cheeks, and kissed her lips.

14

Change of Hearts

In the news:

The 36-year-old leader of Hands with Eyes, Mexico City's largest drug gang, has confessed to carrying out or ordering more than 600 murders, often by decapitation, authorities announced Thursday after an overnight raid.

Scott Daniel Benavidez of Kewa (formerly Santa Domingo) Pueblo admitted to striking a tribal officer with his pickup during a feast-day celebration, hoping to stop the officer from discovering that, contrary to tribal law, Benavidez carried a case of vodka in the truck's bed.

According to the Commerce Department, an unexpected 4.4 percent jump in the US trade unbalance—to $53.1 billion in June—bodes ill for jobs and income in the manufacturing sector, one of the country's last fully functioning engines of growth.

"People keep telling me how excited they are about having a baseball team call Santa Fe home," said Andrew Dunn, founder of the Pecos League. "First, however, the city needs to bend its rules and allow beer sales at a public facility."

By 10:40 the next morning, the temperature outside had climbed past ninety degrees. At Surely You Jest, Candy sat working, as usual, behind her closed door. Down from the long hall's end, five of the press's authors had gathered in the conference room next to Benji's office and across

from Charlie's: Jane and Joe Tash, Vanessa Z. Nord and Seymour Sabatini, CPA Kittie Rehmeyer.

Though the foot-thick-walled room had once served as library in the former Civil War officers' barracks, half a dozen wicker chairs now surrounded a table newly fashioned from cedar planks. For the rare meetings of this morning's size, Charlie had placed a couple of armchairs, saved from his Mississippi home—and reupholstered in red-and-black—in the corner nearest the water cooler. Opposite sat a medicine cabinet, coffeemaker and supplies, and a shelf of Surely You Jest best sellers, half of them penned by Rolf Goodenough.

On a dais Charlie had built, he and Benji occupied the armchairs in twin outfits: loafers without socks, khakis, short-sleeve dress shirts, and the red anniversary suspenders reading *Santa Fe 400 Years* they'd worn to Pranzo Italian Grill almost a month ago.

Charlie crossed his legs. "It's the Possum here who persuaded me to call you last night." He paused to pat Benji's shoulder.

The younger man leaned forward, leveled his granny glasses, and smiled at the group as the fan waving from a shelf nearby blew the end of his ponytail from his back.

"Persuaded me, as my heir, to come clean-o with the five of you. I promised Benji to attempt an explanation without the silences and upsets and weird expressions I love to use. Why you five? Because of all my babies, you're nearest to publication."

He tipped sideways to grasp from Benji's lap a leather-bound binder containing dozens of transparent sheets whose pockets held three-by-five cards. He spread it on his bandaged right forearm and pinched out a card. "When I arrive at seven, my first chore is to shuffle these author cards, prioritizing them according to how much income we're expecting in the mail the following few days. Your five cards I haven't rearranged for, willy-whompers—sorry about that, boyo—probably a week."

Joe Tash shot his hand up. "Listen, where are you going with this? I told Jane, sure, I'd drive her in but I don't have a lot of time. And my bad back won't take this chair very long for palaver." He yanked the Baggie of jerky from his shirt pocket, extracted a piece, and began to chew.

"You're right," Charlie said, though wishing to launch an elbow into the coauthor's temple.

"I'm right about what?" Joe looked at the wristwatch whose frayed band had so annoyed Charlie when they'd met early in July.

"To get on with it." Charlie returned the binder to Benji. "You others met Kittie Rehmeyer, next to Joe there, at the photo shoot for *You Can Save Us All*. We're gonna keep that title, by the way. Kittie is Surely You Jest's CPA, and a fine writer. Though her book on relationships is ready to see daylight, she has some possibly dark news. Then we'll hear from Señor Sabatini."

In spite of the heat, Kittie had decided to emphasize the seriousness of what Charlie had given her permission to share by wearing a black pantsuit and black two-inch heels. She'd meant the lavender blouse that peeked out, like the silk blossom she'd tucked into her bob, to convey glimmers of hope, though at this moment she felt none.

"I'm sorry to report that the press is facing bankruptcy, unless Charlie and Benji are able to find a lessee to replace Sotheby's by October." She waited for the news to take hold, then, "October gives the boys forty-three days, likely not enough time in the down economy we're mired in. Charlie tells me that Seymour may have a different opinion."

On the table's other side, next to Vanessa, the real-estate tycoon from Chicago merely stroked his left mustache, then his right one.

Kittie removed her glasses and set them onto a cedar plank. "Even so, bankruptcy is not the end of the world for us, nor for the boys."

Christ in the barn, Charlie thought, I didn't give you permission to call us "the boys". That Benji finally agreed to spend the night is his and my secret.

Feeling indeed boyish, however—downright frisky, in fact— Charlie stopped twisting his Old Miss ring and glanced over. Benji's face remained impassive, though he brought his thumbs under the red suspenders, stretched the straps, and let them snap back.

"Under the Bankruptcy Code," Kittie said, "Chapter Thirteen allows the debtor to retain ownership and possession of all assets, devoting a court-agreed-upon portion of future income to repaying creditors, generally during a period of three to five years. This would allow Charlie and Benji to continue publishing us, if Charlie can prove he expects steady income."

"Good enough and many thanks, Kittie." Charlie flattened his hand and pushed it toward her. "I own certain rentals beside this building and my assistant, assistant for now, and I have developed a provisional plan. But first an update from Seymour Sabatini."

"Hello." Seymour removed his white Stetson garnished with a partridge feather, and nodded to the group. "Our almighty Pooh-Bah believes I can save his financial posterior, thus helping him concentrate on getting us published rather than lose energy to filling out bankruptcy forms. And now that I have love in my life"—he turned to pinch Vanessa's cheek—"I'm devoting a lot of time to justifying our publisher's faith in my capabilities.

"The upshot, as of this morning, is glum. We thought the O'Keeffe Foundation was a shoo-in; the executive director said two weeks ago that a major benefactor had earmarked half a million to expanding staff for research. Yesterday, sadly, his admin told me the fellow has been diagnosed with cirrhosis of the liver and plans to redirect the money to St. Vincent hospital."

"Saint Victims!" Joe blurted.

"Your call, friend." Seymour rubbed his hands together, then pulled a scrap of paper from a pocket of his guayabera. "So I have three backups to approach, a movie production company wanting a foothold in New Mexico for the tax breaks, a group of lawyers hoping to increase their fees by moving into a historical building near the Plaza, and the Santa Fe Chamber Music Festival folks down the street, who need more room for archives. If I find a lessee, Pooh-Bah promises to publish my second collection before year's end, plus my sweetie's new masterwork."

He reached down to pat Vanessa's buttock through the filmy dress imprinted with chickadees that she'd worn to the Tashes' cover shoot.

"Cupcake," she suggested, "not in public, huh? You embarrass me." But she grinned across at Jane and Joe.

"Joe has to leave, which means Jane, too," Charlie said, "so I'm accelerating this merry-go-round. Benji and I are nothing without you all, also nothing without our art director, the irreplaceable Candy Carlton, who's slaving to keep to our hoped-for production schedule. She, by the way, knows diddily-squat, forgive the expression, about the possibility of bankruptcy. Lips tight, if you will. Three days ago, after Jane and her son left, I boosted Candy's salary."

The front chimes rang, followed by the slamming of the entry door and boots clomping along the plank flooring.

"Chas? You decent?"

At the shout, recognizing the voice, Jane discovered herself trembling.

"Don't let him in here," Charlie whispered.

Benji hopped off the platform as Charlie told the group, "Until my assistant gets back, won't take a moment, I'm going to explain a few other expenses."

Benji hurried into the hallway, coughing at the stench of tobacco.

The cleft-chinned writer in the tattered straw hat stopped two feet away. The tendons in his neck stretched as he peered down. "Where's your boss man, shorty?"

"Meeting with authors. What do you want? You know the rules about appointments." Biting his lip, Benji hauled his ponytail onto his chest.

"Rules be damned. I'm sick of waiting."

"For what?"

"You owe me royalties, bub." Mad Dog grabbed a pearl-handled .45 from one of the holsters hanging from his belt, spun it by its trigger guard, and pointed it at the younger man. He yanked a folded paper from his hip pocket. "I've figured what you owe me just from your statement three months ago. Close to two thousand smackerroos. You write checks like your elder half? That or expect a shoot-em-up here before lunch. You—then Chas. *Comprendes*?"

Benji felt like breaking out laughing. But could the revolver possibly be loaded? What if this crazy old buzzard launched a bullet at his kneecap?

"Whoa, there, big guy. I've signed your checks for the past year. Just signed you another," he lied. "Walked it to the post office yesterday, know-ing we were so far behind."

Rolf's shoulders sagged. He re-holstered the weapon. "Straight, what you're telling me?"

"Would I lie? I'd be a dead man for sure-o." My God, Benji thought, last night, after Charlie signed the papers and later I helped him cum, I'm even starting to talk like him.

The faux cowpoke re-holstered his gun, shifted his shoulder bag. "Gotta give that Christian Science credit for something." Showing a few gold teeth, he wheeled and left, activating the chimes.

"Ah, here's the boyo."

The cushion Benji plopped back onto had stayed warm.

"So, rub-a-dub-dub," Charlie said, spreading his hands sideways, "I've just laid out for you babies our major expenses. Now that my assistant's back, let's face sources of income. To keep turning out top-quality titles, I'm going to need production funds. That means money up front, at least for a while."

"Hold it." Pressing the tabletop, Joe half stood.

"Hear me through, Jane's sahib. You'll have your chance." Charlie paused until Joe sank down. "We've congregated to look the here-and-now in the eyes; no blinkies. I've gotten pretty good at guessing production costs after give-or-take a thousand titles. As of this morning, upfront funding from authors has become mandatory for everyone except proven money machines like Mad Dog Goodenough, however a pain in the ass he is to work with.

"Those who can't or won't pay a couple of thousand or so before Lightning Source churns out finished product will have to step to the end of the queue. Please know I feel bad about that. And I'm downright sick to have to tell you, Jane and Joe, that moving full speed ahead with *You Can Save Us All* is no longer in the cards."

"What? After all we've been through with you? Unacceptable, Mr. Small!" The dangling silver cross that Jane squeezed next to the undone button of her shirt dug into her palm.

"Patience a moment longer. Three big reasons for the delay and note that I'm trying to explain the facts logically. First, the subject matter is too risky, crucial as we've agreed the book is. We've never published a work like yours and our outlets might be wary. Second, it's a long book, consuming valuable time for editing and proofing, though we do, agreed, have a stop-'em-in-their-tracks cover shot, thanks to everyone in this room, and to Benji's D705 digital camera. Third, and perhaps most persuasive, there's no point in giving Surely You Jest money for production, then having little left for promotion. Maximum ballyhoo for *You Can Save Us All* is the key.

"Stay!" Charlie told Jane, who had thrust her briefcase onto the table. "I said you'll get your hour—few minutes, whatever. I want to emphasize this has not been fun." He swiped his forehead with the back of his hand. "Deely dooly, I love every one of you truly, and it hurts. But Benji and Kittie finally put some cockamamie sense into my head. Now—Joe? Jane?"

"My wife," Joe started in but Jane, leaping up, pile-drove him down.

"Foul, Mr. Small! Twenty-four hours ago, across the hall, you gave me a publication date of no later than the second Monday in September, if Joe and I could proof galleys within forty-eight hours. This morning at breakfast, to my shock, yet not really, Joe accepted Goldman-Sachs' offer to return to New York and again light the torch for its commodities department. He says he'll fly back and forth, at least until our reading at Words, Words, Words the last night in September. He's also promised to be our New York City presence, set up readings there."

"Which may be difficult."

"Which *won't* be difficult. He's got lots of contacts through the Yale Club.

"He'll have no time, however," she told Charlie, "to help me proof. As always, the Lord stepped in, an hour ago, Marta Means and my son volunteered. We may have to work all night but we'll do it. Which means—and I hold you to your sense of honor—that you or Mr. LaForge up there with you print out the galleys and hand them over *before you leave for lunch.* The Lord be our witness, Mr. Small."

Jane sat and blew out breath. She forced herself to fold her hands in the lap of cargo shorts matching her husband's, having guessed that the publisher and his assistant would be wearing twin outfits one-hundred percent.

None of the seven present spoke; even the stubby refrigerator next to the coffeemaker grew silent. From outside came the rumble of a truck bearing ice cream to the Eldorado Hotel.

Under the table, Seymour groped for Vanessa's hand and grasped it.

"Choo-choo," Kittie said.

Charlie stopped twisting his lips. "I'm Choo-choo again?"

"Yep, and yike, you know? Reconsider what you said about the Tashes' book. Its message is too important. I'm volunteering to postpone publication of *You Did Good, Girl.* Okay? So you've signed off cover and text, so what? A handbook for gals over sixty on how to secure hopeful relationships? There won't be *any* relationships if a sustainable planet, our garden paradise, wilts under global warming or goes phooey in a nuclear war."

Charlie's mind snapped back to last night, signing the document making Benji heir, their high spirits, the cabernet and after-dinner port, the carnal rightness of what he'd despaired of ever happening. In answer to his ex-wife, he simply shrugged and threw out his arms, while Benji held his bare knees tight, hoping to convey, as future owner, I'm here to listen.

Vanessa's heavy brows touched and parted. "I second what Kittie said. *Roses and Thorns* can wait, too, even if I won't be able to read in October at my reunion." She swept back a mass of hair, uncovering the mole above her eye that Seymour said turned him on so. She smoothed the organdy hiding a hip and, cheeks dimpling, added, "Seymour and I talked with the Tashes after their shoot. He won't mind waiting on his book, either, I'm betting. Cupcake? Let's ask Trevor the Troll to reschedule our readings for December—January, February? My collection and your *Babes in the Woods* premiering after three years in Charlie Small's drawer is not so urgent as what the Tashes are trying to persuade humanity to do, you think? Before we face annihilation?"

She reached over, felt the gray hairs on Seymour's neck needing her razor, and kneaded his wrinkled flesh.

"So good, doll," he whispered.

"If Jane and Joe don't have enough funds to cover production *and* promotion, Seymour will, I'm pretty sure, be able to help out," Vanessa said. "Yes? Now that you've told your Pakistani widow you've lost your appetite for kebob? Because a gorgeous, someday-to-become-a-world-famous poet named Vanessa Z. Nord has stepped into your life, you lug—and her astrologer confirms it's an okay match, Pisces and Leo, age spread doesn't count?"

Kittie's silk blossom shook with her bob as she smacked her hands together. "What a gift you are! How could any man say no?"

"Certainly not this hombre." Seymour wrapped Vanessa's shoulder and she hopped her chair as close to his as she could.

"Riddly ruminators, then, shift into high gear with the major effort. I'll figure the Tashes' upfront check this afternoon."

Charlie pressed both sides of his hair, shaped and re-dyed two days ago. With his left arm he pushed down on the chair's and rose. "*Truth, independent of doctrines, knocks at the portal of humanity.* I'm more a schizophrenic than scientific Christian, but Mary Baker Eddy was so right on. My babies! Shoo, hop, go, before I break into tears."

He flapped his palms forward. "Jane, Joe, give Benji half an hour to have your galleys waiting. Treat yourselves meanwhile to the new Alfred Stieglitz exhibition at the O'Keeffe. Superb-o, Benji tells me."

"Can't you just e-mail galleys to my processor at home?" Joe asked. "New York wants to hear from me."

"Use your iPhone. I want those galleys in my hands," Jane said.

Charlie settled back as Seymour, Kittie, and the Tashes followed Vanessa into the hallway. The entry door closed behind them, unleashing the chimes.

Charlie pulled out his father's pocket watch, replaced it, smiled at his nails, curled and straightened his fingers to relax them.

In the emptied room, "Hey, bud, " Benji said.

"I need some quiet, Possum."

"Yeah, fine, but I did a pretty good job on those fingernails of yours last night, hey? Even though at first I thought, What the hell?"

"Everything changes except Infinite Mind, boyo."

15

You're Mine

In the news:

Thirty-two suicides last month set a US Army record. The service began releasing figures in 2009, even though reducing suicides was made top priority in 2004. The Army's previous record for self-destruction was 31 in 2010.

The median cost of a cyber crime has risen to $5.9 million, compared with $3.8 million last year. Costs include money spent for security experts, loss of productivity, software upgrades, and value of stolen intellectual property. The number of attacks has risen 44% in the past twelve months.

Women who smoke are 25% more likely to develop heart disease than men who smoke, according to *The Lancet*. For data, researchers surveyed four million smokers across 50 years. Women account for one in five of the world's 1.1 billion smokers, and almost one in three tobacco-related deaths, such as cancer.

Fifteen-and-a-half-foot marine reptiles called Plesiosaurs probably gave birth to single, five-and-a half-foot babies, researchers report online in the current issue of *Science*. Marion and Charles Bonner discovered an adult pelvis sticking out of northwest-Kansas shale, where the possible fetus's pelvis lay buried. Fellow Kansan paleontologist Mike Everhart wonders, however, how such an assumption as single birth can be made from the only two Plesiosaurus fossils ever found.

It was nine o'clock on the Saturday morning following yesterday's meeting with authors to come clean on Surely You Jest's probable bankruptcy. Benji had just stuffed into his pocket the green ribbon imprinted *draft-dodger runaway* with which he'd secured his ponytail after breakfast at Charlie's. The office floor fan caused his loosened hair to dance about the collar of an orange shirt matching his boss's.

From across the counter, Charlie ducked right and grabbed Short Stuff, who lay curled on top of the fax/scanner. "Catch!" The cat's mews morphed into a drawn-out yowl as he tossed her to his assistant.

Short Stuff, bell jangling, hit Benji's chest with a thump. The cat's bony shoulders started shaking as Benji cradled her in one arm. "What the hey, mister, you gone nuts?" Benji bent to set Short Stuff at the end of the counter where her food and water dishes waited.

"I've paid in pain for my entertainment, Possum." Rubbing his still-bandaged wrist, Charlie returned to the chair under the photo of Benji's father. His wrist continued to burn and he shook it. "I've been wanting to sling that calico since we met three years ago. But boyo, oh, boyo, you're moving in. Welcome to the Las Campanas wildlife preserve and a second childhood for me for sure-o." He jabbed the pinkie holding his Old Miss ring toward the man nearly forty years his junior.

Benji hauled out the reefer he'd rolled this morning in Charlie's bathroom, and a matchbook lettered *Pranzo Italian Grill*. His hand trembled as he fitted the doobie's end to his lips, wondering how his boss would respond.

He'd lifted the hand to light a match when the septuagenarian leaned forward and swatted the matchbook from his grasp. "No smoking here! Bumblecock and moonshine, no smoking pot anywhere I'm around."

"Thought I'd run a beta test, Charlie. I need to keep a few pleasures if I'm to come live with you."

"Blackening your lungs isn't one of them."

"And Short Stuff?" Benji asked.

"What about her?"

"Part of the package, bud."

As though in response, the calico commenced to rattle her kibbles and nose about the dish.

"We'll find a way to deal with your pussycat."

"Not by throwing her around."

Charlie fixed his gaze on copies of correspondence and invoices from suppliers awaiting filing, stacked a foot high in the corner behind Benji. Last night, as during the previous two, the boyo had held him in his arms until he'd slept. Longing to restore the tranquility of that, Charlie said, "Possum? Let's hustle over to Starbucks for a couple of nonfat Caffé Mochas, hold the whipped cream."

"Fine. But I need to get clear. What's in your head about a timetable?"

"Timetable?"

"For moving to your place."

"Ay-es-ay-pee."

"I'd have to break a lease, Charlie. There are penalties."

"You heard the Tashes. They agreed to pay three thousand upfront for their tome. "If, contrary to what I said yesterday, I surprise Kittie, and Seymour and Vanessa, that we intend to open the throttle on getting their efforts into print, I betcha, crack my nuts, they'll cough up two grand apiece."

"Rushing like that means a lot more stress for us."

"Whoever said shoot-for-the-moon standards aren't a slew more work? But shifting into hyper warp for Seymour and his dollface should guarantee his finding us a lessee. Ducking-out-of-your-lease penalties?" Charlie aimed his thumb at himself. "Ask Mister Moneybags, boyo."

"First- and last-month at seven-fifty a pop because of Short Stuff, forgo the security deposit of a grand, and we're watching twenty-five hundred big ones sucked down a black hole."

Charlie slapped his chest, hoping to stem the wheezing that had begun.

"That's the sound of laughing away twenty-five-hundred bucks Surely You Jest could use? When in four months I can move free of charge? That's dumb, Charlie. Start treating my cat right and I'll keep spending two or three nights a week with you, not a problem."

Benji bent to lift Short Stuff from the dish of water she was lapping and hugged her. They watched Charlie's face rise above the counter.

"You're getting cold feet!" The publisher's forehead had reddened.

"I'm trying to talk sense, mister. Why would I back out? I have your promise in writing that when you've vanished from mortal view—and we both believe that's in a distant future—the company and your rentals are mine. Last night all you had to do was lie back and let me bring you off. Before you know it, I'll be available *every* night. We'll learn how best to take care of each other, no? Meanwhile, I may want you to paint over the walls of your casita. That white's too damn stark."

"Come around the counter so I can see all of you."

"Why?"

Charlie waited for his wheezing to lessen. "I want to share a tale."

Benji eased his five-legged chair past the fan's whirling blades and parked beside the fax/scanner. "Go ahead."

"In 1971, Andy Somers, the ad manager at Continental Can, and I left New York City for two weeks' R&R up the road at Bishop's Lodge. Where I spotted an advert in our all-the-news-not-fit-to-print *New Mexican*. High Desert Books was for sale."

"You've told me this many times, Charlie."

"Bet not why I needed the rest so badly."

"Andy said keep working a sixty-hour week and in two years he'd see you got his job, something like that. But you wanted to break with him. Your offer for the press was accepted and you renamed it how your uncle responded on finding your dad a suicide: 'Surely you jest'. Close enough?"

"I didn't only *want* to break with Andy, boyo. I was desperate, and here's why. I discovered he was bedding the skirt recently tapped as executive secretary to the Can's chief financial officer. Plus, I was still legally leashed to Old Miss's prom queen. She'd learned of my man-to-man liaison with Andy and decided to sue for alimony.

"But the main reason I felt impelled to leave New York and Mississippi behind? We'd just lost my kid brother."

"You had a brother?"

"Mam delivered Clive at age forty-one. We lost him in manhood to a tractor. He'd been drinking. Driving it, he fell sideways, the tractor's wheels kept rolling, Dad figured the left rear must've squished him. Would have been your age. Understand now why I want to keep you by my side at night? Riddly ruminators, I think the asthma's gone." Charlie pushed his shoulder blades against the chair's oaken back.

My life's become too weird, Benji thought, and clenched his eyes. But, Mother, you know what? I like playing footsie with this old guy. We have the same ambitions and sexual equipment. No chance of bringing offspring into this rundown world.

"Charlie," he said, "I've printed out a check for Mad Dog Goodenough, one *you* oughta sign, restore Rolf's confidence in the press. Like to get it to the PO before we hit Starbucks."

At eleven that same morning, Candy turned her convertible off Bishop's Lodge Road onto the lane just south of Tesuque that Hercules had said led to his casita. Was she crazy to be doing this? Following the traded shouts with her husband an hour earlier, she'd decided to call the number Herk had urged on her after he'd fallen from the wall outside her office. She'd kept it unused in her wallet for more than a month.

The little Miata stumbled over ruts until Candy spotted the meadow he'd described, Marta Means's mares and gabled home to the left, aspens and cottonwood fronting the Tashes' hacienda. How sweet the air smelled! The sun heated her scalp through her straw hat.

Crows beat their way up from the cottonwood as she turned into the graveled, semicircular drive. She stopped beside Herk's red pickup, and finished her can of Pepsi.

When she'd phoned, wondering if he might have time to brainstorm ideas for *You Can Save Us All*'s design and cover, his enthusiasm had spurred her to dab Leonard's fifteenth-anniversary gift of Dior's lily-of-the-valley scent, Diorissimo, behind her ears.

Stupid, she thought, though a spotted towhee's trill lightened her self-doubt. Wondering if the Tashes were home, she opened the car door, lowered her clogs to the stones, reached back to slam the door shut, and carried her portfolio toward Herk's flagstone porch.

"Hola!" A paint-splotched smock hid Herk's shorts and most of his black tee. "Thanks for wearing pink — my all-out favorite color. And for looking great in capris. C'mon in." He swept a blond-haired arm behind him.

"Remember, this is a business call, Herk." She paused under an arbor laced with wisteria, leafed but blossomless in August.

"Doesn't mean I can't appreciate chic."

"I'm easily ten years over your radar." But she could feel herself blushing under the cropped blonde hair she'd decided to shampoo after he'd urged her to stay for lunch.

He stepped to the side and she passed into the room. "Oh, my!"

Next to a window facing his folks' carriage-house-become-garage sat a stool and easel. A canvas leaned against the framework lit by two halogen bulbs. Part penciled lines that needed filling in, part acrylic, the painting showed a clump of willows dipping like women washing waist-long hair into a creek backgrounded by a flowered slope.

"Right behind my folks' place, on Little Tesuque Creek," Herk said behind her. "Had to Google *wild iris* for the blossoms' shades of blue."

"Serious talent in classic bachelor's pad," she murmured. "Except for the swivel chair and workstation. Like mine at the press."

"I grab design jobs wherever I can find them."

She took in the rumpled quilt thrown on the bed, the card tables holding sponges heaped in baking pans, the jars of paint, piles of rags, spray bottles, yogurt tubs stuffed with Popsicle sticks and palette knives and brushes, the armchair's cushion flattened under avian and botanical reference books. Pre-gessoed canvases angled against the wall. Even the dining table bore watercolor pencils and a stack of sketchpads opposite the knives, forks, glasses, and paper napkins folded for his and her meal.

"The place needs a woman's touch." She blinked at its overall odor of salsa.

"Your touch?" He stepped close but kept his hands off.

"I'm married, Herk."

"So?"

She laughed, removed the hat, swiped a palm back over her hair, and held the hat against her thigh. "That fan feels good."

He pulled a folding chair away from a table stationed near the window, waited in silence for her to sit, then took the chair opposite, facing the easel. Sitting so close convinced him that, as after climbing the wall, he had fallen for this chick.

"No one to bother us," he said. "My mom and Marta Means, my stepdad, too, finished proofing the galleys at one o'clock this morning. They've taken Marta to La Plazuela to celebrate. So. How can we do our part to help make their dead-tree effort to save the world a runaway best seller?"

"You're hilarious, you know that?" Candy brought her portfolio to the tabletop and unzipped it.

In half an hour they'd settled on mixing Old Style and Modern typefaces on the cover—Garamond to convey the longevity of the problem, Bodoni to convey the need for immediate action—and Times New Roman for body text to show breadth of application.

Candy closed the portfolio, twisted toward the fan, wiggled the neck of her shirt to attract the cool air. She turned back to smile. "We've done it. Not an angry word. I'm used to tempers flaring: Charlie, my husband."

"Because why? You and I click." He gazed at her face, clean of lip gloss or eye shadow.

She realized her bladder hurt. "Use your bathroom?"

He gestured past the ironing board, laden with shirts and a couple of khaki shorts, which pointed toward the doorway.

Upon emerging, she startled—he was standing against the jamb.

"Scare you?" he asked.

She backed toward the dining table. Drat, her stomach growled. She hoped he didn't hear.

She bit her lip as he approached. How he towered over her own five-foot-six! He gripped her right hand and wrist.

"Hercules, please, let go."

"I want some information."

"Make a little room, will you?"

"Sorry." Sounding as shaken as she felt, he released her, leaving on her wrist a circlet of heat. He moved to the end of the dining table and sat. "Come closer, okay? I won't touch you."

"Criminy, Herk, information? What kind?" She took the cater-cornered chair.

"I'd like to know what the emotional bond could possibly be between you and your husband."

"I told you. We fight. Fighting's a powerful bond."

"Fight over what?"

"Who's going to buy the lactose-free milk, who forgot sardines. Why did he, why did I, leave the hand towel crumpled on the counter. You name it."

"You met how?"

"American Academy of Child and Adolescent Psychiatry held a convention in Albuquerque. Big-time, pro-bono client for the guy who owned the ad agency I started with after college. Leonard was president of the southwest chapter. My boss called him creative, could give me ad-campaign ideas. Leonard was older, and dumpy, and he drank too much. But starry-eyed Candace wanted children right away to please her mother, diagnosed with Parkinson's the week before. I figured, as a dad, a child psychiatrist would be totally low-risk."

"Plus he made one hell of a lot of money."

"Plus he made more than a lot. Are we through?"

"Why no kids—am I right?"

"His enthusiasm vanished as soon as we married. For all bedtime activities. And my best friend had had a lousy experience adopting. Look, this is making me very uncomfortable."

"He's got you where he wants you."

Her stomach growled and she stood. "Herk? I think I better go. Thanks for the time." She turned to collect her sketches and notepad and portfolio.

"You said a few days ago you can't afford to leave him."

She faced him again and cupped her hips with her palms. "After you left Tuesday, Charlie gave me a raise. I told Leonard that night, said maybe we ought to split. He closed himself in the den to enjoy, what, Internet porn? Desk-drawer gin? Before he left this morning, to deal with what he calls 'Medicare and Medicaid drudge,' he started shouting—I'd explained he'd have to fix his own lunch today. He accused me of having another affair."

"Another one?"

"In addition to my pathetic sexual escape with the owner of the ad agency, six months into wedlock."

Herk jumped up. "Candy!"

Her hands flew to her breasts.

"Leave him. Let him flounder."

She stayed planted, inhaling his scent as his arms wrapped her and he crushed her lips against his.

She pushed at his rib cage until he backed away, and managed to reach her portfolio. How clammy its handles felt! She stuffed it full.

Now she began to laugh. "Hercules, oh, dear Hercules, oh, my. I am leaving here, though, you see?" She jammed her hat onto her head.

"Leave *him*. Not me. I've got green-chili enchiladas in the fridge for us, fresh from Tesuque Market."

"I can't take more right now of whatever these feelings are all about, Hercules."

She hit the corner of his bed's frame, ducked to rub her shin, jerked the front door inward, slipped past, and left it open. She hurried to the Miata, hoping he was following or about to call from the stoop. But no sound came.

Hardly had she wrenched the wheel to head south toward home than she'd determined, in spite of her grumbling belly, to speed directly to Leonard's office and deliver the coup de grâce. Loneliness be damned. Let him swear off the booze, let him plead.

How good the breeze felt! She should leave the top down more often.

By the time she reached Calle Medico twenty minutes later, half a mile from the three-bedroom adobe they'd owned for thirteen years, her mind had refilled with anxiety. "So I have to keep buying groceries every other week?" Leonard had yelled. "Keep phoning the handyman? The electrician? The plumber? The roofer? Sweep the garage? I make six times the income you do. Why should I keep demeaning myself?"

You explained why last week before passing out, Leonard. You need to reward your filthy-rich self with martinis and wine, and cordials after dinner. Sick, so sick. And me? Sicker. Or am I too judgmental? Maybe you and I simply need a vacation. You can afford to give us two weeks in Florence or Siena. I'll talk to Charlie after *You Can Save Us All* appears next month. I will do that.

She fit her Miata into the slot facing the scraggly elm, and the rabbitbrush beyond. Despite the deodorant she'd rolled on after breakfast, her armpits felt sticky as she dropped her portfolio from the passenger seat down to the floor mat.

She left the roadster, bent over to release its latch between the two seats, pulled the black top forward to the windshield, latched them together, locked up. But whose was the beat-up sedan, left taillight dangling by a wire, parked next to Leonard's BMW? A pair of knitted dice hung from the jalopy's rearview mirror. Leonard hadn't mentioned a patient; he claimed he never saw patients on weekends.

She hurried past the Russian olive looming over shades, drawn against the heat, of the soundproof sanctum next to his office that Leonard had created for parents and their children who needed private crying time.

The two-toned electronic bell dinged under the ramada when she pulled the glass entry door open and stepped in. A woman in her mid-twenties, Candy judged, sat in front of the poinsettia Leonard always kept in the waiting room at the near end of the hall. Bare thighs crossed, she held one of the glass table's *Elle* magazines on her lap. Rag dolls, stuffed pandas, and koala bears waited for hugs in a basket near a wooden box filled with Legos. The woman's snub nose increased the seeming size of her bubble cut, a few strands from which straggled across her forehead and temples. A silver ring, encrusted with bits of what Candy bet were colored glass, encircled her right forefinger.

Leonard's office door was shut at the hall's far end.

"Hi, there!" said the woman and licked a chapped lower lip.

"You are who?"

"My daughter's in Lenny's care."

Her voice resembled a mouse's squeak. "Lenny?" Candy echoed.

"Dr. Carlton. Who are you?"

"Dr. Carlton's wife." Candy marched across the Navajo throw and proceeded down the hall.

"He's in session!"

Behind her, Candy heard the slap of the magazine thrown against the pile of others, then the woman's footfalls.

She wasn't fast enough, however, to stop Candy from opening the door.

In contrast to the sanctum—furnished only with a sleeper couch, low mahogany table, and makings for coffee and tea—Leonard's office held his desk and floor-to-ceiling bookcase, a red-and-blue-and-yellow fiberglass table, matching chairs, and two armchairs. Her husband sat in the one under his certificate from Columbia and three drawings he'd asked Candy, years ago, to create. The female figure leaping from a boulder represented the Id's leap of faith; the male rushing toward her represented the Superego's warnings; and the Russian wolfhound framed between these—staring into the room, tongue lolling—represented the Ego.

When Candy burst in, the eight-or-nine-year-old at the table tightened her arms around a stuffed shark. Her head started to jerk and she lowered her chin toward the top of the bathing suit she wore. Her flip-flops began tapping the carpet.

Leonard pulled off his tortoiseshell glasses, overturned his notebook onto his thigh, and, in suppressed-anger monotone, asked Candy, "Can't you see I'm working?"

Before she could think how to respond, the voice close behind her squeaked, "I told her, Lenny."

"'Lenny, Leonard? What's going on here?"

"Patient confidentiality, Candace, please. Go home, prepare a cool drink, and I'll join you in a bit."

"This is 'Medicare and Medicaid drudge'? Some kind of code?" Candy jerked her chin sideways to blurt, "Take your hand *off* me," and reached to pry the woman's fingers away from the neck of Candy's tank top.

"Don't be afraid, Lily." the girl confided to her shark. "It's just warmed-over Mommy and Daddy. Before he left to be happy. You and I won't fight ever again, will we, no way. Lenny promised to sew back the fin from your tummy that I tore off."

"Not exactly, BeeBee. What I promised was—Candace!"

His new tone startled her out of trying to believe the reality she found herself in. "You did get my name right, Leonard. A welcome beginning."

"Go!" His sideburns and double chin shook.

BeeBee jumped up and pointed the wounded shark's nose at Candy like a tommy gun.

BeeBee's mother pushed Surely You Jest's art director aside to face Leonard at the room's far end. "What's the matter with your wife? You told me—"

"What did he tell you?" Candy nearly shouted.

The woman grabbed her daughter's shoulders, propelled her and the shark forward, and clutched the still-sitting psychiatrist's hand.

"Huh?" was all Candy could think to say. Then: "I won't be home tonight, Leonard. Doing Jemez Hot Springs or Red River. I'll call you tomorrow before my piano lesson."

She let loose a belch before wheeling.

16

No Way Gay

In the news:

"Endless war" is how Americans tag reality these days, according to military historian Eliot Cohen. A decade of conflict in Iraq and Afghanistan has crushed the "smug certainties" that the US could bludgeon enemies into swift surrender. Adds Lt. Gen. David Barno, "Today's Army lives in a bubble separate from society."

Post offices have hit hard times. The postal service is running $9 billion above its $67 billion-a-year budget. Tax money no longer subsidizes it—postage fees do. Postmaster General Patrick Donahoe wants to cut costs by closing 4000 post offices and retiring a third of its 660,000-person workforce.

A wildfire in central Texas has raced across seven miles in 40 minutes to destroy nearly 500 homes, a state record. Since the fire season began last November, this wildfire is only the latest among 63 blazes that have consumed 3.6 million acres. "We have exhausted our resources," says a spokeswoman for the Texas Forest Service.

About 1,700 years ago, a gladiator school flourished 28 miles east of Vienna. Mapped by radar, the school, rivaling in size the famous Ladus Magnus of Rome, remains underground, pending excavation plans that allow maximum conservation. The doomed men lived in cells barely big enough to turn around in but could pamper themselves in baths.

Three-and-a-half weeks had passed since Charlie told the Tashes, Seymour and Vanessa, and Kitty Rehmeyer that he needed production funds upfront to continue publishing their manuscripts. He'd also spread the word to a couple of dozen other authors, half of whom had him return publishing rights to them.

By Tuesday, September 6, the extreme heat of August had dropped by a good ten degrees. Near noon, Charlie and Benji waited to take Benji's mother to lunch at Amaya Restaurant in the 51%-Picuris-tribe-owned Hotel Santa Fe.

The two men occupied high-backed, oak-framed chairs at a granite-topped table closest to the teepee that dominated the lawn behind them. Their napkins perched upright like red-cotton flames. Two already-filled water glasses sat beside outsized, tan-colored menus while flute music and the smell of meat grilling pervaded the room. A woman, whose face resembled crumpled parchment, and a man in a sombrero, whispered two tables away. A party of four sat outdoors under a *latilla* overhang.

"You brought the stevia?" Charlie asked.

Benji hefted a hip and exposed two purple-and-white packets. "Sweetener at the ready, boss, but look—can't you ditch the Sherlock Holmes's cap?"

"Nope." Charlie drew a hankie from his slacks' pocket and wiped the back of his neck. "Hot."

"Mother doesn't even expect you to be here. It's me she drove down to talk to."

"Figured you needed protection."

"Bullshit. You're afraid I'm not going to tell her I've committed to come live in your casita. Dammit! I gave you that cap as a joke to wear at photo shoots."

Charlie winked, flipped his finally healed right wrist, and gave Benji the finger. "Holy moly guacamole. Our ball-breaking poetess approacheth." He waved frantically toward an oaken podium.

The Picuris hostess led Jeannie toward them as Charlie whispered, "Let's eat fast."

Benji stood, saw his mother glance at the white socks and sneakers Charlie had insisted they wear, along with the fawn-gray knits labeled *Armani* that he'd bought Sunday at the Discount Center. Benji stretched out his arms and Jeannie, bending forward but keeping her hips distant, let him hug her.

"Hello, Mr. Small. My son didn't mention you'd be..."

Charlie rose and peeled his checked cap off with both hands. "Where the Possum goes, I follow."

"It's 'Possum', still, is it? I thought we straightened that out on my last trip down. His name is Benjamin, remember? Though his father does say Ben."

Benji opened his mouth to comment but smiled instead, shrugged, and sat.

Charlie crooked his finger at a full-bellied, aproned waiter emerging from the kitchen. From a tray, the Native American set bowls of soup and a basket of bread in front of a couple holding hands. He lowered the tray to his thigh and approached Charlie, Benji, and Jeannie.

Continuing to stand, Charlie fitted the cap back onto his head. "My companion and I will have the Cobb salad, two ice teas, and two-percent milk. Jeannie, any idea what you want?"

"May I get comfortable first?"

"Deely dooly, forgot my manners. Here's a menu. Can recommend the Cobb. Or grilled salmon, why not?"

Jeannie descended, smoothing her skirt beneath her. She moved a pinky down the list of offerings, then looked up. "Portobello and zucchini sandwich, I believe. Coffee black."

"*Benjamin* has sweetener if you need it," Charlie said to her.

"There may be enough stevia for three." Benji pushed at his granny glasses and addressed the waiter. "Add a cup of your cream-of-broccoli soup to my salad, will you? And a side of sweet potato fries."

"Just the salad's fine for him," Charlie said.

"I'm starving, Charlie!"

"And I'm your watchdog, boyo."

"Mr. Small, what gives you—"

"Two Cobbs," interrupted the waiter, "two ice teas, two two-percents, one portobello-and-zucchini, one black. And a water."

"No water for me," Jeannie said.

"We're in a hurry." Charlie sat again. About to place his hand on Jeannie's wrist, he decided probably not such a great idea.

Jeannie's seven bracelets clinked as she set her beaded purse on her lap. She pulled a tissue from the pocket of her blouse, a pink-and-red-blossomed hand-me-down purchased Saturday at the flea market on the Taos plaza. Blotting her nose, she said, "It looks like I'm going to need to talk to both of you, doesn't it?"

Charlie stared across.

"Benjamin tells me that you've made him your heir."

"Right you are."

"I'm assuming that means he'll be able to share in whatever profits the press makes?"

Charlie stared.

"I know it's going to mean longer hours."

"Where are you taking this, Mother?"

"In a minute. First I wish you or your employer would fill me in some. When I called last week about coming down, you said that the sky was brightening in terms of finding a replacement for Sotheby's Realty."

Benji glanced at Charlie, who merely shrugged. "Two lessee possibles, Mother. One of our authors, from Chicago, who has his New Mexico real estate license, thinks we'll know by October."

"Good news, isn't that? Such glum looks, you two. And the big book project?"

"To save the planet?" Benji asked, to clarify, as Charlie started twisting his Old Miss ring.

"You were so keen about it when I visited in August," Jeannie said.

"The coauthor husband has returned to New York. But the son's set up a website and the wife's building her presence on Twitter and Facebook. She's hired a book reviewer to increase her hits on Amazon and other URLs. The wife's neighbor is booking readings in San Francisco and Chicago and Seattle, we understand. The launch in Santa Fe takes place at the end of this month. What else, Charlie?"

"Beats me. Where's that chow?"

"In fact," Benji went on, sounding for his mother, he hoped, like a publisher-to-be, "we're accelerating schedules of a dozen or so authors because they've agreed to pay production costs up front."

"Why, Benjamin, that's wonderful! Just as you suggested on my last trip down."

"Indeed."

"Well, listen to that. Your father's word. Talking more and more like him. Such optimism. Though of course his hair's already gray." Jeannie peered meaningfully at the sienna-haired Charlie, who merely raised an eyebrow before unfurling his napkin. "And managing your own weight so nicely."

"I'd as soon you didn't compare me with Dad, Mother." In fact, he thought, I need to take down that photo of him in my office.

"Your father does seem happy enough, heading up peacetime nuclear projects before his retirement from Livermore in January. He married his live-in girlfriend six months ago—but you must know that."

"Not a clue."

"Don't you call? Do you write?"

Charlie drove his fist down, though the white tablecloth muffled the smack. "Christ in the barn, woman, no doubt for sure-o you'll be penning poems about all this, but don't approach Surely You Jest for publication, all right? What in buggeropolis is it you're dancing around with us? Ah, finally. Provisions."

Belly ballooning his apron, the big man with the black braid brought their teas and the coffee, set miniature pitchers down. "Salads and sandwich lickety-split." The strings of his apron bounced as he headed back.

Charlie ripped open the two packs of stevia and dusted the white powder over the ice cubes, first in his glass, then Benji's. He poured half a mini pitcher of milk into each. "Well?" he asked Jeannie.

"Just a minute." She sipped her coffee, then faced her son. "Benjamin? "You're going to need to take more interest in your children."

"And why is that, Possum's mam?"

Jeannie jerked her head around. "I'm not talking to you. I'm thanking you to let me finish without interruption."

She turned toward Benji again. "A week ago, Marian spent three nights in the psychiatric ward—I drove to Denver to help with Meadow and the boys. Their mother's not doing well. She's drinking much too much, Benjamin. The doctor on duty told me the tests showed liver damage. And a week later, Meadow was found in the girls' bathroom smoking marijuana."

"I smoke marijuana, Mother."

"Stopping when you move in, boyo."

"Move in?" Jeannie asked.

"To my casita. Soon, Benji's mam, very soon."

"Benjamin?"

"Not exactly sure when, Mother."

At this she smoothed her palms along her bare thighs. "Why, every time I see you—yes, I know, so far only twice—are you and Mr. Small dressed exactly alike?"

"Soul mates," Charlie answered.

"That's what you're calling this relationship?" she asked, returning his gaze.

"I believe that's what I said."

"You're old enough to be his father!"

Benji felt ants crawling along his legs.

"Gobbledegook and who's the crook? And your son's young enough to be my dead brother. Irrelevant, lady. Age doesn't exist."

"Oh, yes? 'Soul mates' implies what?"

"*Let Truth be proclaimed,/ Let God's love be retold,/ That men of good will/ May their brethren uphold.* A hymn from my upbringing. You note 'men'? Note 'brethren'? Nothing here about women. Nothing about age."

"You and I are heading toward *ancient*, Mr. Small. The undersides of our arms are wrinkling. Our double chins are dropping toward triple. We dye our hair. You want to build the illusion of youth? Pluck the white from your eyebrows, like I do."

The waiter reappeared as Benji decided the time had arrived to come clean.

"Sandwich here," Jeannie said. "Cobbs there."

The Native American set his tray on the table nearby and brought their plates over. "Gentlemen, madam. Do save space for dessert."

When he'd left, heading for five women the hostess had just seated, Benji screwed up his courage. "Mother? Charlie and I are best friends. We're also, as Charlie likes to put it, man-to-man lovers, in the process of learning what the other gets pleasure from. Can you accept that?"

Jeannie's head jerked sideways. For a moment, her lower lip engulfed the thin upper one. "No, I won't and I *cannot* accept that. You who sired three children, who need their father's emotional and financial help, now proclaim yourself gay?"

"Whoa, there, Benji's mam. The term you used doesn't apply." Charlie curled his fingers to examine his nails.

"What in hell *does* apply?"

"Willy whompers, woman, I've told you twice. Best salad in Santa Fe, yummy, yummy, blue-cheese crumbles, you're missing out, Jeannie." He speared a tangle of lettuce, impaled a hunk of grilled chicken below it, and thrust the fork into his mouth.

Jeannie scraped her chair back, reached for her purse, and rose.

"I'm sorry, I've lost any stomach for this restaurant's delicious-looking, portobello-and-whatever-else treat. I *am* your mother, Benjamin, and I forbid you to live with this person."

Charlie pulled down the front bill of his cap. "Do I feel a breeze blowing?" He stacked another forkful from his Cobb. "Possum, dig in, hop, hop, we need to hustle-o back to the office."

But Benji wasn't through speaking. "This 'person' you're telling me to stay away from, Mother, helped me sober up, start losing weight and learn to work hard, start sending payments to Marian. Charlie doesn't like 'gay'? Doesn't like 'old'? Poof! Mortal errors. Those words no longer exist."

Jeannie leveled her forefinger at him. "What you need to do this weekend is to drive to Denver. And begin wiring at least *twice* as much money as you have been to the family you abandoned."

"You're out of your gourd."

"Oh, no, oh, no, you don't talk to your mother that way."

"Keep ragging me and, far as I'm concerned, you're history."

She audibly sucked in air, then turned to Charlie, who kept on munching as though she'd left long ago.

"You see, sir? What you've done to him? Benjamin is *not gay*. He has three children. My son is homo—*heterosexual*—and you, Mr. Small, are I-don't-know what. Monster comes closest, I'm quite sure."

Ten seconds later she was hurrying between the room's bar and red willow partitions toward the oaken doors leading out.

17

Red Flag

In the news:

The intensity of the decade-old war in Afghanistan is growing, not abating, according to UN Secretary General Ban Ki-moon's latest quarterly report. The average monthly number of armed clashes, roadside bombings, and other violence stood at 2,108, up 39 percent from a year ago, though the US-led coalition disputes these figures.

Deaths from prescription drugs have passed deaths from car crashes, as well as deaths from heroin and cocaine combined, according to the US Centers for Disease Control and Prevention. Experts say the prescription addict is increasingly white, suburban, and upper-middle-class, mostly teens stealing parents' meds, and elders hoping to reduce pain.

The FBI has arrested Rezwan Ferdaus, 26-year-old Northeastern University physics graduate, for plotting to blow up the US Capitol and the Pentagon. Ferdaus told agents posing as al-Qaida members that he planned to load small aircraft with G-4 plastic explosives, and use GPS equipment to fly them remotely into Washington.

The 1914 baseball card of Babe Ruth, arguably the greatest slugger in history, is now worth perhaps $600,000, according to the director of the Babe Ruth Museum in Baltimore. Ten such cards exist; in 2008, one sold at auction for $517,000. Only the 1909 T206 Honus Wagner card has drawn higher bids, valued today at more than $2 million.

❖ ❖ ❖

On Friday, September 30—launch date for Jane and Joe's *You Can Save Us All*—the maximum temperature of seventy-six was six degrees less than three weeks ago when Charlie and Benji met Jeannie LaForge for lunch.

The 6 pm cloudscape outside Trevor Quesenberry's bookstore stopped even Santa Fe's Friday night gallery goers, used to such displays. Before entering Azul Fine Art or Grimmer-Roche for wine and canapés, many of them gawked at the salmon-, rose-, and lilac-colored swaths imbuing the cumulus mounting above the Jemez, and above the ski basin to the east.

Inside the bookstore, the corner platform between orange and green walls supported a lectern, folding chairs for the coauthors, and a glass-topped table holding a glass of water, a hardback of *You Can Save Us All*, and a handheld mic. Tunes from *The King and I*, arranged for strings, drifted over Joe and Jane, Herk, Candy, and Marta in the front row of folding chairs, with perhaps thirty more warm bodies scattered behind them.

Trevor filled Styrofoam cups between the coffeemaker and espresso machine. This evening's crackers, Swiss cheese, celery, and carrots were also available gratis; a few patrons took advantage of Trevor's generosity by overloading their paper plates.

In front of the kiwa fireplace stood a doublewide card table. Copies of the Tashes' book lay waiting for sale, $29.95 for the dustjacketed version, $22.95 for the soft cover. Both featured Benji's black-and-yellow MINI Cooper surrounded by Surely You Jest authors hoisting chapter-head signs. Subheads reading *Reverence for Life* and *Detach with Love* slanted across the cover's lower half. Above the title, in elegant Bodoni, appeared the words, *A How-To Book of Survival*.

All copies featured back-cover blurbs by Marta Means and Lester R. Brown. Soft-cover copies of the latter's *Plan B 3.0, Mobilizing to Save Civilization*, stood upright for sale nearby.

Arrived from New York last night, Joe leaned across Herk to address Candy. "You're telling me that Charlie Small and his minion or heir or what-the-hell, after their Wizard-of-Oz rhetoric, don't plan to show up tonight?" From his short-sleeved button-down he took the Baggie of mesquite-flavored jerky, opened it, reached in with his teeth to clamp down on a strip, stuffed the Baggie into the pocket of his poplins, ripped the strip in two, stuffed part back into his shirt pocket, and began to chew.

"Less noise, can't you manage?" Jane whispered.

"The guys mostly don't attend readings, Joe," Candy said, dressed for this evening in a ponderosa-green sheath. "Their usual excuse is they have no energy left after the day's stressors, though Benji did phone about tonight. He asked if I could represent the press, make an apology. Sorry, guys, not my job."

"I phoned Candy, too," Herk said. "She's leaving her husband—did Mom tell you?—when she can find a place to land." He threw his arm around the art director's shoulder. "Like to believe she's sitting here now because of me."

Candy had decided to forego perfume, not wanting Herk trying quite yet to press her into spending the night. He had picked her up where she waited in her Miata in the Women's Club parking lot near her home.

Unlike Candy, however, Jane had gone all out, dabbed on Cartier's Kiss of the Dragon, shadowed her eyes, glossed her lips, and left her amber hair loose over the frock displaying honeysuckle blossoms that Joe so liked. A silver cross hung between the buttons of her cardigan. So far, sadly, Joe had given no sign that her efforts pleased him.

Now Rolf Goodenough appeared through the glass door beside the fireplace. He marched down the center aisle created by the facing ends of the rows of chairs. Straw-hatted, cuff-linked in a Tattersall shirt, and smelling of tobacco, he squatted beside Jane. "Go to it, gal," he said. "Any trouble, you shout for the marshal, hear?" He lifted the bronze star pinned to his leather vest.

"Can you believe that Mr. Small and Benji don't plan to come?" Jane asked.

"You betcha, missy. Why I'm here for support."

"How did your late-August Tea Party Roundup go?"

"Three people showed. Guess Santa Fe isn't ready to host us yet. Hi, you," he said to Marta.

Hearing the ragged voice, Marta peered past Candy, Herk, and Joe. Her breasts bulged like papayas, half out of the knit's scooped neck. A white knit band propped her black curls up.

"Looks like we're about to deal the first hand," Joe said. "Here comes Quesenberry of the streaming hair."

Jane and Herk turned, saw Vanessa—followed by Seymour and Kittie—pull open the door Rolf had come through. They waved and took chairs eight rows back, near the Children's Corner.

Seeming to float in his flared-bottom slacks, Trevor shook several hands as he approached, causing one of the blouse's unbuttoned cuffs to flutter.

More people pushed through

The buzz of the crowd grew louder.

"Jane!" Joe snapped.

"Don't yell at me."

"You still reading first?" Joe asked. "Maybe I should."

"And why is that?"

"I thought it might help my back."

"Aren't you using the Yale Club's gym?"

"No time. Go ahead first as we planned."

"Ho, you two." Trevor took Jane's hand, reached for Joe's but Joe withdrew it.

"Big crowd, read loud. All righty, follow me." Trevor tossed one side of his hair over his neckerchief and headed for the platform's steps.

After Jane and Joe had seated themselves next to the lectern, Trevor picked up the mic and in his high voice said, "Thanks a bunch for coming — Lordy, what a mob. I'll wait till you settle down.

"Tonight is perhaps one of those cornerstone events that change history. Think back to Allen Ginsberg's nineteen-fifty-five reading of *Howl* at San Francisco's Gallery Six." Trevor lifted *You Can Save Us All* and wiggled it so the jacket would flash reflections from the ceiling's recessed lights. "This major effort to alter the thinking of our planet's seven billion souls came about, as great undertakings do, from Jane and Joe Tash's personal tragedy. Our authors lost a daughter to a head-on."

As some in the crowd drew in their breaths, Joe whispered, "Where'd he get permission to say that? You?"

Jane wagged her head, pulled a tissue from her purse. "Marta, probably."

"Lesbian whore."

"A bit of business," Trevor continued, squeezing the loose knot of his neckerchief. "Restrooms are past the Children's Corner. You'll find coffee, tea, cookies, and punch behind the spinners. Words, Words, Words, named in honor of Hamlet, the Gloomy Dane, offers refreshments at no charge during key events like these. In return we ask you to consider buying a book, maybe two. And now, one of this high desert Shangri-La's local notables will introduce our featured speakers." Trevor gestured toward the first row. "Marta Means."

Marta grasped Candy's hand, rose, hurried to the steps and up, filled her lungs, and took the mic. "I'm going to read a bit from—"

A bruiser of a man she'd never seen, wearing a business suit, stood at the end of the row opposite Seymour, Vanessa, and Kittie. He made a megaphone of his hands to shout, "Louder!" His cheeks seemed as inflamed as his Windsor-knotted tie. Next to him perched a birdlike woman with a pink peony pinned to the lapel of her jacket.

"How's this?" Marta held the mic close.

"You got it." The man's bald head gleamed.

"I know him from somewhere," Jane said to Joe.

Seymour, draped in one of his guayaberas, used Marta's momentary silence to tell Kittie, "May have found our publisher his lessee this morning. Say a prayer."

"Shhh!" An old woman with forget-me-nots in her French twist turned back toward the platform.

"How I'm going to proceed," Marta said, leaning forward, "is read a short paragraph from this book's preface, give you thumbnails on our authors—who moved here from Connecticut last January—and then hand the evening over to them. Afterwards, you'll find copies of *You Can Save Us All* near the fireplace, along with Lester Brown's 2008 classic, *Mobilizing to Save Civilization.*

She reached into her miniskirt's pocket for her reading-glasses' case, extracted them, stuffed the case back, put them on. "From the preface: '*In the three years since Brown's book appeared, the problem has gotten worse. We face universal extinction, at least nasty mutilations, when Armageddon erupts. But* You Can Save Us All *offers a multitude of easy-to-apply solutions which*"—here Marta removed her glasses—"you'll hear about presently.

"Jane and Joe lost a daughter to the high-speed products of our materialistic society. It's why they swore to devote their lives to writing and promoting this book. They wrote little before it, nothing since. Joe earns his keep by ensuring that commodities like soybeans and orange juice and poultry stay available for our well-being."

"I do?" Joe wondered as his gut spasmed, causing him to swallow what was left of his jerky.

"Jane, my dear friend, spends all her time setting up publicity and readings for the book. Imagine the strain she and Joe are putting on their marriage to get the rest of us to change our ways. I believe I'll stop here. Jane?"

Marta hugged her neighbor before clambering down the steps and retaking her chair next to Candy.

Herk leaned over. "Loved how you described my stepdad's work."

"I'm going to tell the truth up there?" Marta said. "We want to sell merchandise."

Sitting behind, Mad Dog clamped her shoulder. "Best quiet down."

"Good evening," Jane began. "Can you hear?"

The bald man in the suit said nothing. But a goateed gent wearing a roadster cap aslant called, "With you all the way. God bless."

"God surely does, sir," Jane said. "We have an entire chapter on how closet prayer, prayer circles, and church, synagogue, or mosque can speed the work we need to do. For those not given to praying, my husband has a chapter on how any large group, this one tonight even, can effect positive change.

"But talking about God or no God often stirs negative emotions. So I'm going to read from Eight. It deals with—"

The suited man jumped up. "Let's hear the chapter on prayer. My wife and I did not lose bucks on our house in Palo Alto to try this berg out for size just to lose the Lord."

"I begged you not to order wine, Jonathan. Please." His wife tugged his elbow, squinched close-set eyes as he swatted her hand away.

"You and I," he yelled, "traded talk after church last Sunday. Let's hear it for God."

Jane held the flaps her dress collar closed and bent down. "Holy Faith, Joe. The gentleman worked for Hewlett-Packard. Head of human resources, I think. Complained about taxes on his golden parachute. What'll I do?"

"Run."

"Sir," Jane said into the mic, "I want to read from a nonreligious chapter because most of our book's suggestions do not require faith. We need help from nonbelievers as well. Chapter Eight offers ways to dress, in order to brighten our outlook and the outlook of others."

"Loving the Lord needs to be a part of that."

Rolf twisted his head to face him. "Amen!"

"Beginning of a donnybrook," Joe commented to no one.

"Jonathan, I'm leaving," squeaked the wife.

"I have the keys. Sit down."

Marta looked back. "Buddy, you want God? Buy the book."

"Muzzle thyself, lesbo," Joe muttered.

"Oh, Joe..."

"You'd better start reading," he said.

Jane pursed her lips as though to whistle. The book started wobbling. She laid it back on the lectern and clamped the corners with her palms. *"Chapter Eight. How will what we wear, to instill joy in ourselves and others, contribute to saving our planet from collapse? The key is joy, nonerotic joy, we quickly add. Seeing each other in garb that fits well, utilizing colors that harmonize and jewelry that adds spice, but does not bellow greed, beams energy toward the tasks—"*

"Beams energy? Bellow greed? There you lost me, chickie." A gallery owner in the fourth row grabbed a coral-encrusted purse and blue hat from the next chair. She edged her way into the aisle and hurried toward the registers and the front door beyond.

The suited man rose. "Can no one speak for entrepreneurs? God-fearing innovators keeping America in the swim to kick ass?"

Marta jumped up to summon Trevor.

"Finish it, will you?" Joe told Jane. "My back's killing me."

Mad Dog stood and tongued into his cheek the wad of spearmint he'd been chomping. "Kemo sabe? God's on our side, I'm with you. But He wants you now, and I want you now, to zip the lip and give our gal"—Rolf thrust his thumb over his shoulder—"some Good Book courtesy."

"And you're just who, big mouth?"

"I'm so sorry," the man's wife called out. "He promised to stop drinking after we moved. It shortcut his career and he keeps refusing help. Come on, Jonathan, we're going."

"The sooner the better, friends," Trevor said, arriving at last. "We'd all be endlessly grateful."

"Yeah?" Swinging his arm, the man connected with Trevor's chest, knocking him into Seymour's lap.

Seymour eased out from under the storeowner's bulk as the wife, having gained the aisle, played tugboat to her husband's barge, yanking him toward the store's rear. Rolf and Herk followed, in case she required brawn to persuade him out.

Candy ran after them, and wrapped an arm around Herk's waist. "Hercules? It's too much. I need you to drive me back to my car."

From the platform Joe asked Jane, "What are we doing here?"

"Groups Build Leverage, Joe. Stand up and read."

Trevor, having regained his feet, pushed his sleeves above his elbows and addressed the crowd. "Those who attend our gatherings regularly know that this sort of unpleasantness is never welcome and rarely takes place. Thanks a bunch for staying. All righty, Tashes, you're on."

Jane punched Joe's hip with the heel of her hand. He rose and shifted weight to his right leg to ease the pain that sprang from his bunion. "This excerpt is from a how-to guide for building power through group cooperation. I'll read the first few paragraphs."

Jane threw her arm up to steal the mic. "Then we hope you'll enjoy talk and treats. And of course that you'll ask us to sign a book, or several to stash away for Christmas. Joe and I will be over at the table to answer your questions. Or merely to say hello."

"Why extend the torture?" Joe whispered as she returned the mic.

"*Groups Build Leverage,* he said too fast. *"Chapter Three. We'll find much strength in numbers. Witness what Gandhi achieved before Pakistan and Kashmir sheared off. Here are ways to intrigue your fellows into banding together. Use social media to…"*

A couple of white-haired men in the third row, one bearing a neck brace, stood up. Between them they hoisted a woman in capris and a sleeveless tee younger even than Vanessa. The man with the neck brace saluted as they crab-walked into the aisle and fled.

After Joe had thanked the audience and taken his first sip of water, a third of the crowd had vanished. The evening saw the sale of seven paperbacks and two hardbacks of *You Can Save Us All,* and three paperbacks of Brown's *Mobilizing to Save Civilization.*

18

Money Talks

In the news:

Spending by American consumers has withered under rising unemployment and sinking home prices. Which is why visitor bureaus are courting shoppers from overseas. Chinese worldwide spending rose 39% in 2010, followed by Brazil's 30% gain. At the Fashion Outlets of Las Vegas, shoppers from China, Malaysia, and South Korea have driven tour-bus business up 300%.

Defense Secretary Leon Panetta warns that Israel must restart negotiations with the Palestinians, as well as restore relations with Turkey and Egypt. Though Israel maintains a military edge in the Middle East, that's not enough to secure peace, Panetta claims.

Hundreds of villagers are stuck on rooftops northeast of Manilla. Typhoon Nalgae, leaving 59 dead, is now whirling over the South China Sea toward southern China 230 miles away, delivering winds of 75 mph and gusts of 93 mph.

More than 600 pilots from around the world, owning 550 hot-air balloons, are participating in Albuquerque's 40th Annual Balloon Festival. A balloon from Lithuania got caught in power lines, causing an outage at some traffic lights, but no injuries were reported.

At 9:15 on the Monday following the Tashes' reading, lightning crackled and rain beat down on the tar-and-gravel roof of Surely You Jest's conference room. Joe had returned to his suite at the Yale Club in New York. Jane, Herk, Marta, Rolf, and Kittie, Seymour and Vanessa, sat with cups of coffee or tea at the cedar-planked table, while Charlie and Benji occupied armchairs on the dais. Behind her door at the hall's end, Candy was reworking the cover for Seymour's latest poetry collection, *Babes in the Woods*.

"You are the chosen ones," Charlie began. He opened the leather-bound binder holding three-by-five author cards. "I'm glad my heir could reach you all Saturday evening. Before you arrived this morning to learn why he called, he ordered one hundred copies of your upcoming titles, except *You Can Save Us All*. For that world-changing work—disregard Friday night's threadbare sales—Possum told Lightning Source to print up *two hundred* soft covers and *a hundred* hard covers. Marta, by the way, when can you get us typo-free text of your memoir? I've moved your card to the front."

"Not until spring, I'm afraid, Charles. I'm rendering it into couplets."

"More poesy to deal with? Back it goes."

"Choo-choo?" Kittie asked.

"What?"

"A hundred copies of *You Did Good, Girl*? Even at my author's discount of fifty percent, I can't pay you right now."

"No matter. Infinite Mind took charge when our benefactor and his poetess treated us to lunch. Seymour and Vanessa, step up here."

After Charlie and Benji had filled the emptied chairs at the table below, on the dais Vanessa leaned over to kiss Seymour's cheek, then flashed an emerald-encircled diamond to the others. "Tell them, cupcake."

"We're engaged."

"No, I mean yes, but the ring says that. Tell them the news they're waiting for."

"I'm happy to report that, as of November first, we have a lessee to take the place of Sotheby's."

"Oh, whoa!" Marta cried out. She and the authors at the table broke into clapping.

"There's a lot more," Vanessa said. "Share our plan, Seymour."

Jane squeezed Marta's wrist. "You aren't going to believe what's coming, darling. Herk and I promised Mr. Small's assistant to keep our lips sealed."

Seymour smoothed forefinger and thumb in opposite directions over his split mustache. "The Santa Fe Music Festival folks will start filling Sotheby's emptied offices here in two weeks. Their head honcho and our own mighty Pooh-Bah signed a two-year lease in my presence Saturday morning."

Vanessa placed her palm on the back of his neck. "Now I'll tell, and I'm glad the group's sitting down. This dear old guy wants to bankroll a tour of the United States for *You Can Save Us All.*"

"All expenses paid?" Kittie blurted.

"Oh, yeah," Vanessa said. "And Charlie and Benji have agreed to step up production for anyone who's willing to get on board. We start this afternoon to schedule readings. The deal is that, out of the thirty or forty minutes we're given to read to an audience, the host bookstore or museum or environmental organization lets us follow the Tashes with ten minutes for our own book, and after questions, push the sales of both."

"Sounds like a logistics nightmare," Marta said.

"No," Jane told her.

"No?"

"Herk?"

"I've agreed to stick around as Seymour's online organizer, not go on tour."

"I kinda doubt anyone can schedule the larger stores before Christmas," Rolf said.

"Wherever we can't pin down a date before the holidays, our benefactor says he'll pay for readings afterward. Cupcake?" Vanessa pinched his earlobe. "Share why you've become Surely You Jest's deus ex machina. What you told me yesterday after I brought you breakfast in bed."

"Six years ago I started writing poetry. But most of my life I've spent accumulating wealth and making women feel bad about themselves. I'm resolved to leave a different legacy. Thus what my angel just said. Submit your receipts to Herk."

"Except Joe and I keep paying the guy who's writing Internet reviews," Jane said. "From now on, whoever sets up readings, as Vanessa described, gets their book reviewed at no charge."

Charlie added more to the rainy morning's good cheer. "Part of the miracle Seymour didn't mention is that Surely You Jest no longer needs to ask for funding up front. This apparent change-of-course is an act of Spirit, babies, real and eternal."

"Cut the hogwash, Chas."

"Rolf? You can't accept that Seymour's offer is a gift from the Lord?" Jane asked.

"Or swallow this, oh treasured golden goose. My heir and I apologize publicly for not making an appearance Friday night. That bald bastard embarrassing the Tashes was unacceptable."

"You and your sidekick could have stopped that?" Rolf asked.

"Maybe they couldn't but we can. At every event on tour, we'll have a bouncer in place," Vanessa interjected. "Seymour even insists on one at my fifteenth reunion at Laguna High."

"Me! I can do that." Mad Dog knuckled his chest. "Not my style to throw wet blankets on a crusade. For our gal Jane here's readings, I bounce for free."

"Not sure I want you along, Rolf."

"Jane and I will do just fine keeping things simple, pal," Marta said.

A sudden crash silenced the cross talk.

"Wacky woo, boyo, what in cockamamie hell?"

Benji pushed backward, overturning his chair. He dashed across the hall into the mailroom, where raindrops beating the roof seemed louder. The window painted black, which faced the parking lot reserved for Sotheby's, lay in shards over the press's Formica counter. Under the corner of a tarp, a four-drawer filing cabinet butted into the open space framed by spikes of remaining glass. Outside, a branch waved from one of the Russian olives sheltering Candy's walled mini-courtyard.

The art director had run down the hall. Braced by the leg she'd set behind her, she watched Benji use the whiskbroom and dustpan he kept handy to sweep away Styrofoam bubbles and cardboard dust left after wrapping packages.

"Away, babies, we'll be in touch," came Charlie's voice from the conference room.

As the publisher headed for the hall, Seymour called from dais, "Hold up a moment, everybody. Vanessa and I are Command Central. Pull out your pens. Here's my e-mail address. And my iPhone number. If you get voice mail but need immediate feedback, try Vanessa's phone. Give it to them, doll."

Candy had returned to her office when Benji raised his hands to Charlie's tee, blue like his own. "No need to go in, bud—the mail room's cleaned up. Someone with Sotheby's moving a file cabinet must've slipped in the downpour."

Charlie stared past Benji's shoulder at the shelves of warehoused books turned gray by the overcast light, and the window's jagged opening beyond.

"The counter's still damp," Benji added. "I'm heading to the john for towels."

While Mad Dog exited past Charlie and Benji without comment, the rest hung around in the conference room sharing thoughts.

The entry chimes rang, rang again. Charlie turned to face Sotheby's managing director hurrying toward him. A nylon hat hid the Swede's blond locks except for strands plastered across his cheekbones. Taller even than Rolf, he had the hands of a basketball star, and extended one. "Awfully sorry, Charlie. You bet we'll pay for the mishap. I'm trying to get our people out of your hair double-quick in spite of the weather."

Letting the other's hand hang in the air, Charlie waited until it dropped. "Have you and I agreed to restart a conversation? My memory is we've not."

"Excuse me?"

"Fiddlefart, there's a whole gang in there"—Charlie arced his thumb toward the conference room—"ready to help me toss you out. Rub-a-dub, Monkeyshines, hop hop."

19

Sex and More Sex

In the news:

Letter to the Editor: Most of us know that free trade increases the nation's wealth, that Medicare and Social Security are consuming the federal budget, and that minimum wages boost unemployment. Yet recent studies disclose that only 13% of us agree with 95% of climate scientists—human beings are causing global warming. —MaeEllen Strand

Thousands of pounds of discarded clothing, debris from food wrappers, bottles, cans, and other garbage litter a 68-acre site known as Hobo Hill. Rains wash human waste and trash onto surrounding streets, creating stench and a health hazard. "The squatters always come back; they'll tear down a fence to do it," claims Land Use Department Director Ernest O'Toole.

The President has been pushing for a $443 billion jobs plan to be paid for, in part, by a tax on the wealthy. Republicans are resisting. Thus the three-week-old Occupy Wall Street movement, begun with young people pitching a tent in Zuccotti Park opposite the New York Stock Exchange.

Thirty-four-year-old Jessie Garcia has been slapped with a felony charge following his accosting the woman parked next to his car with a sword pulled from a bamboo cane. "I'm a violent man," Garcia told police. This is his fourth arrest in the past decade.

Three days after the joyful Monday morning at Surely You Jest, the Sangre de Cristo Mountains received their first snow. Candy left at three to join Herk for a ride up Hyde Park Road to view the two inches fallen at the ski basin. They planned to buy skis on the weekend.

Five o'clock found Charlie in Benji's office, occupying the armless chair under the photo Benji had taken of Short Stuff to replace the photo of his father. He and Charlie were dressed in long-sleeved crewnecks—one maroon, one olive—for dinner out.

Benji paused from scratching Short Stuff's tummy to pick his lighted reefer from the ashtray he'd brought to work. Narrowing his eyes behind granny glasses, he dragged deeply, held his breath, and pushed it out in an audible *whoosh*. He returned to attending the calico, wiggling his pinkie for her to grasp.

"You know what, bud? I never thought I'd see you allowing an end-of-day smoke in these hallowed quarters."

"I've told you before, boyo, don't treat as gospel everything I say. Mumbledee bandersnatch, we're celebrating. Marta's somehow secured a Barnes and Noble reading next month in Chicago? Plus, you've said our Mad Doggie has lined up Bozeman, Casper, and Salt Lake, and that, at her reunion, Vanessa's agreed to read from the Tashes' tome as well as from her own *Roses and Thorns*. Everything's coming up roses. It seems Mary Baker Eddy was right on this one, and I attempt to quote: *Harmony in mankind is as real and immortal as in music. Discord is unreal and temporal*. But I am concerned about that tum-tum of yours. Pull up your shirt."

"C'mon, Charlie."

"Those twelve-step meetings for fatties you're attending—are you, anymore? Next I'll discover you've returned to swigging vodka fizzes. Give me a look-see."

"Didn't you get enough look-see last night?"

Charlie sprang up.

"Someone will spot us!"

Charlie closed the shutters over the fax machine, where Short Stuff lay purring. Before Benji thought to back out of reach, the septuagenarian lifted the younger man's shirt. "As I figured. Spare tire even when you stand. I love you anyhow. Kiss me."

Benji returned the embrace, meeting Charlie's cracked lips full on.

"Damn it to pieces, Possum, let those gorgeous locks flow."

"Now?"

"Down, down, I want to show you off tonight." Charlie reached behind Benji's head, held his ponytail in one hand while rolling off the elastic band. "Spread it out."

Benji fluffed air into the auburn sheaves now reaching his shoulders. "Charlie—"

"Shhh." Charlie flipped a forefinger to his lips, slid it off. "Let us hie to Rio Chama for some osso buco and chocolate fantasy. Then fly home for more quality time in the hay, what I'm re-dubbing my—*our*—wildlife preserve."

"Where do you get the energy?"

"Teaching you a lot of tricks, am I? Get that cat into its carrier."

The phone on Benji's desk rang.

"Leave it."

"Only means I'd have more to deal with tomorrow." Benji dragged from his doobie, stubbed it out, twisted the end, and pocketed the roach.

Charlie stepped aside as Benji leaned forward to lift the receiver.

"You've called Surely You Jest. How may I help you?"

"Mom said I could reach you," a husky voice replied. "Is this you, Daddy?"

Benji recoiled as though struck by a whip. "This is Meadow?"

"Daddy! Mom's gone bughouse. Can't I come live with you? I'm going to kill myself if you won't take me. You have to do it. I love you, Daddy."

"I can't talk with you now."

"But I'm your daughter!"

"Call me tomorrow."

When she started screaming, Benji hung up, thanking the God he didn't believe in that Charlie had let him smoke the weed.

"Your hand's trembling, Possum. That was—"

"My fourteen-year-old."

"I warned you to let the phone be. Ask yourself, Am I living the life that approaches the Supreme Good? Yes, I am. Am I demonstrating the healing power of Truth and Love? Yes, yes, and yes. Pay her no mind. What's she want? Don't explain now. Let's hop."

At the same hour, ten miles north in Tesuque, Marta sat across from Jane at the Tashes' kitchen table. The wind blew fitfully, causing a branch to tap the window that looked at blossomless iris fronting the meadow of Bermuda and buffalo grass.

A strand of the hair Jane had left loose snaked across the page of the notebook spread in front of her. Dressed in a paisley skirt and green jersey, she sipped from a tumbler of homemade limeade.

"Foo, everything's become so strange—good strange, darling." Jane lay down her ballpoint beside the bouquet of silk poppies, and half rose to kiss Marta's cheek. "It's unbelievable: You helping me, Candy divorcing because of Herk, Joe doing who-knows-what three-thousand miles away. And the reading dates piling in! I do hope they don't mean more disasters. Poor Seymour—the bills."

Marta rubbed the bare skin of her thigh where barbed wire had torn her jeans. "Our big-bucks guardian angel seems happy enough to be so involved. Seymour understands how important your book is." She drew her palm back and forth across her turtleneck. "This memoir you're working on, too. Dealing in a page-turning way with Tatum's death, with Joe finking out to leave you and me freedom to explore a life together." Her forefinger hit the outline Jane had been scribbling down. "Be sure to leave space for how you told me you plan to deal with your church and the Tea Party."

"You see I'm not wearing a cross."

"Such a beautiful blouse." Marta ran her palm along the sleeve's flowered rayon, shoulder to wrist.

"Oh, you. Don't worry. If you love me hard enough, I'll be explaining that the certainties of Episcopalianism, and the Tea Party's rules for returning to a simpler life, just don't work for me anymore." Jane snuffled, pulled a tissue from her skirt, and blew. "But how sad, Marta."

"*We're* not."

The lid of the pot heating on the six-burner stove began to rattle. "My green chile stew—it needs an hour to simmer. Have I ruined it? What'll we feed Hercules and Candy?" Jane ran to turn down the flame, went to the Sub Zero to remove the cooled plate of bell peppers, chiles, and diced potatoes, and dumped them into the broth and cooked pork.

"Candy and Herk are so grateful to you, they won't care what's for dinner. Let's give your outline another half hour."

Jane returned to the table, cocked her head at the whistles and trill of a White-crowned Sparrow. "This land on the creek is so blessed. I do hope I can come live with you, make a new beginning. Even if you are my neighbor, it's such a change."

"For the better. Gets you out of this house, its memories of Joe. If you and I don't work out—but we *will*—you can always move back. Phillippe is maintaining our grounds. Wherever you end up, let's see if we can pool funds for Greta to add a few nights of cooking to her housekeeping, once we're back from book-touring."

"I can't wait to go, Marta. Isn't it Detroit where we're stopping first? Maybe *You Can Save Us All*'s suggestions will help the city fathers learn how best to rebuild.

"Do you really love this blouse?" Jane pinched its collar. "Want to know what I love?" She arced a hand to flutter Marta's black curls. "Imagine, cuddling together every night. Oh, how embarrassing!"

"Embarrassing?"

"I'm wetting."

Marta laughed. "You sweetheart."

"Should I free Joe from his promise to read in New York City? I'd be far more comfortable reading on my own."

"Tell him that, unless he threatens to stop covering your mortgage. I'll be in the audience wherever you are."

"Dear Marta. We're so lucky. I only joined the Tea Party as a result of Tatum's..." She slapped her notebook shut. "I can't focus with you so close by. I'm going to go cut some wild grasses and get rid of these phony poppies."

"But they're lovely, Jane."

"They're fake."

While Jane gathered stalks of plains lovegrass from beside the front steps, Candy and Herk lay twenty yards away on his bed, behind the casita's heat-trapping shades. Her cargo shorts, panties, bra, and tank top draped his *Botanicals of Northern New Mexico* and a reference book on southwestern butterflies, scattered with his own clothes on the throw he'd picked up at the flea market in Chimayo.

"Hercules! Shame on you, exhausting me." She cupped her pubis, then squirmed closer, pressing against his ribs. "Let's shower together. Can we shower together? Leonard never wanted to. He said he couldn't get clean enough with me there in with him."

In the false dusk, Herk twisted his head to glance at the clock. "We've got an hour." He shifted to fondle one of her breasts.

She stroked his hand. "Can we make love again before we shower? It's been such a long dry spell for me." She pulled away and searched for his genitals. "Want some coaxing first?" Leaving the rubber on, she began to knead him. "Isn't everything working out? Your mother renting me her house for the cost of the mortgage after she moves to Marta's. The readings getting set up."

"Doesn't mean sales will improve. The book's still pie in the sky in my opinion."

"Maybe. But so what? Everybody's happy, looking forward to life again."

"I'm having trouble paying attention, Candy."

"Good!" She released his erection, flipped to her back, started beating her arms like wings across the sheet. "*All* of us are angels, even Charlie, finally able to help authors he's had to neglect. A changed man."

"For now, anyhow. But he and his boy toy better learn the fine points of online publication. The books they're used to producing are dead trees."

"Realist." Candy waved her arms faster, then shifted to her side and reached to palm Herk's buttock. "Charlie talks about his bubble world; let's enjoy ours. Hey! Have you got any bubble bath?"

Herk shook his head.

"Then lie back and let me do my thing."

Readers Guide

1. Have you a favorite character? Who? Why?

2. Which character do you love to hate most? Why?

3. Do you believe books like *You Can Save Us All* can change the human penchant for destructive behavior? If not, why not?

4. Have you had any experience with a book or eBook publisher? Please share.

5. Have you known anyone troubled by her or his sexual identity? Describe. What was the outcome?

6. Do author Michael Scofield's attempts at humor work for you or not? Cite two examples.

7. How does Scofield treat serious belief systems like Episcopalianism, Christian Science, and the Tea Party Patriots? Would you rather he had dealt with these topics is a different way? Why?

8. Does Seymour's offer to pay all expenses for a national reading tour seem realistic? Has anyone ever unexpectedly helped you out of a financial jam? Describe.

9. The last section in Chapter 15, titled "You're Mine," takes place in the office of Candy's husband, a child psychiatrist. How believable do you find the scene, based on experience you've had with a therapist?

10. It does seem probable that Joe and Jane will be going separate ways. What three reasons can you give for this? How important a factor is Tatum's death?

www.ingramcontent.com/pod-product-compliance
Lightning Source LLC
Chambersburg PA
CBHW031331060726